Atomic
Love

Atomic Love

A Novella and Eight Stories by

JOE DAVID BELLAMY

The University of Arkansas Press
Fayetteville   1993

97   96   95   94   93   5   4   3   2   1

Designed by Gail Carter

The paper used in this publication meets the minimum requirements of the American National
Standard for Permanence of Paper for Printed Library Materials Z39.48-1984.   ⊛

Library of Congress Cataloging-in-Publication Data

Bellamy, Joe David.
      Atomic love : a novella and eight stories / by Joe David Bellamy.
          p.   cm.
      ISBN 1-55728-277-3. — ISBN 1-55728-278-1 (pbk.)
      I. Title.
    PS3552.E532A94   1993
    813' .54—dc20   92-39315
                                                                                        CIP

For
my brother Jimmy
(1928–1977)

and for
Reynolds Price

Eve Blachman

Marriott
Residence Inn

Eve —
Thanks for
the loan

David

Acknowledgments

The stories in this book derive entirely from my imagination. Where I have occasionally used real names or what seem to be physical descriptions of real people, it is done purely in the interest of fiction and is not intended to portray the actual lives of any real people, living or dead.

These stories originally appeared in the following magazines:

"Sunoco," in *Story*
"Atomic Love," in *North American Review*
"Saving the Boat People," in *Ontario Review*
"Make Love Not War," in *Prairie Schooner*
"Times Square," in *Mid-American Review*
"The Weeds of North Carolina," in *Kansas Quarterly*
"Roth's Deadman," in *Nebraska Review*
"Beautiful Vases," in *Ploughshares*
"Bloomville," in *Ohio Review*

My thanks to the National Endowment for the Arts, a federal agency, to the CAPS program of the New York State Council on the Arts, to the Kansas Arts Commission, and to St. Lawrence University for grants or awards that helped me to complete some of the work presented here; thanks also to the editors of the magazines where the stories first appeared.

Contents

Sunoco

Jocko had a bad habit of cruising along at about eighty-five in his Gran Prix, and if anyone got in the way he would close in on their back bumper like some gigantic shark ready to swallow their tailpipe. When the driver of the other car finally noticed and swerved out of the way, we would swoosh on by as if we had important business in some other state. Why he never got caught, driving that fast, I'll never know. I was trying not to pay much attention to it. I had my hand under Nadine's blouse in the backseat.

My half-brother Jocko and his newest wife Gloria were up front, and Gloria was humming a little song with the radio and bopping her head to the music. Gloria worked as a bunny at the Playboy Club in Cincinnati. She was a short girl with a blond beehive and big boobs, and she liked to lead Jocko around by the nose. My date Nadine was Gloria's younger sister. Nadine had dark hair and eyes and extremely sexy lips. Overall, she was not as cute as Gloria or one other girl I liked in Yellow Springs, where I went to school, but she wasn't that bad either. She was okay. She was growing on me.

Nadine was in Cincinnati visiting Gloria, and Jocko and Gloria thought they would fix her up with me, since I was home from school and about her age—I was twenty-one then—and not doing anything that night. So we had had this boring dinner at some fake-swank restaurant full of artificial palm trees, cocktails and steaks and after-dinner drinks, with Jocko presiding in his gaudiest blue-glass tie-pin and cuff links that winked and glittered in the lights every time he raised his fork or sipped his scotch. Then Jocko had driven us back to their little brick house in the suburbs, weaving and speeding like a maniac out Columbia Parkway in his new Pontiac.

As soon as we got in their house, Jocko started pouring drinks for the four of us. We sat around the living room for a while trying to make

1

conversation, then Gloria said she was going to slip into something more comfortable, if we didn't mind; and Jocko went into the kitchen to make some more drinks. After a while Gloria came out in shorty pajamas—and maybe I should have gotten the hint and left at that point—but when she saw that Nadine and I were preoccupied, she joined Jocko in the kitchen. I didn't know what they were doing out there, but they had the radio turned up and they seemed to be talking hotly, and rattling ice cubes, and getting louder and louder, ranting at each other.

They had been married for about six months, and Jocko was in charge of used car sales at Honest Rocky Labaron's Pontiac in Sharonville. For him, it wasn't a bad job, all things considered, including the brand-new cars he got to drive; and with Gloria's extra income from the Playboy Club, you'd think they would be doing okay. But it sounded like they were arguing about money, and I know that Jocko wanted her to quit her job, for obvious reasons, and that Gloria didn't want to quit.

Nadine was sitting on my lap, but she was one of those girls who was afraid you wouldn't respect her afterwards if she did anything more than kissing on the first date. I liked her well enough—she seemed kind and sweet—but I thought she was pretty silly. Still, she was trying to tell me things with her tongue that were far more eloquent than anything we had yet managed to say to each other with words. Each time we would come up for air, she would look deeply into my eyes and shake her head and sigh audibly as if she really couldn't believe her conscience had to be such an obstacle—because this was definitely a situation when she would like to make an exception. It was a nice gesture, and I appreciated it.

We were doing a fair job of blocking out the fight that Jocko and Gloria were having in the kitchen, but suddenly we heard a loud bang and the sound of glass scattering and raining on the floor in the other room and then Gloria screaming. As I got up to see what was going on, Gloria nearly ran over me on her way to the bedroom. She bumped into the coffee table, then gave it a good kick, screamed "ouch," and hurried into the bedroom and slammed the door.

Jocko was standing under the fluorescent lights in the kitchen, looking sheepish and dabbing at the blood on his chin with a balled-up napkin. He gave me a mischievous little grin. As soon as I saw him, I thought maybe she had ripped him with a steak knife or I-couldn't-imagine-what. His white shirt had blood all over it, and he had a bloody streak on his cheek and a gouged-looking place on his chin that was dripping blood in a steady stream.

"Are you all right?" I said.

"No problem," he said. "I never liked this shirt anyway."

He was a mess, and the broken glass was lying all around his shoes and sprinkled on the counter and across the table. I grabbed him by the shoulders and started to turn him toward the doorway, where Nadine was standing.

"What happened?" Nadine said, her face registering several stages of alarm as she took in Jocko's cuts and all the blood.

"The goddamned glass just popped," Jocko said. "You never saw anything like it."

"I'll get a broom," Nadine said.

"Let's go into the bathroom, Jock, and get this cleaned up—what do you say?" We started trudging unsteadily together toward the bathroom.

"What's wrong with Gloria?" I said. "What happened, for God's sake?" I got him in the bathroom and turned the cold water on and wet a washrag and dabbed it carefully at his chin.

"Must have been something I said is all. Who knows? The next thing I know her glass is bouncing off the wall. Ban-go!"

"Did she throw it at you?"

"No, she just threw it. You know. Women. She'll get over it."

"You want me to go talk to her?"

"No. She's probably packing her bag or some damned thing."

"This chin looks like it could use some stitches."

"Naw—just a scratch—don't worry about it."

"It's still bleeding like a bitch."

"The Band-Aids are in here somewhere. Just put a good Band-Aid on it. That'll fix it."

I located the tin box of Band-Aids in the medicine cabinet and tore open the biggest one I could find and stretched it out across his jawline and pressed it down. I tore open another one and lined it up next to the first. The blood seemed to be slowing down. I opened a third and crisscrossed the other two parallel to his lip. He checked my handiwork up close in the mirror. The cheek was not as bad, just a slice along the surface. I didn't see how it could have happened from splattering glass; it looked too straight and long. "Are you going to be all right?" I said.

"Hell yes. Let's drink to it."

"Maybe you'd better change your shirt—get a clean one?"

"Naw—it'll dry."

"Maybe I'd better go home."

"Well, suit yourself, pal."

"I think I will."

Jocko wagged his head and sighed, and his gray eyes unfocused for a second. He put his boozy, mutilated face up close to mine and whispered: "This is what women will do to you, Mike." Jocko held out his hand to show me he also had an ugly gash across his thumb and wrist.

"You'll live," I said, unwrapping more Band-Aids. His big hand palm up reminded me of when he used to give me bubblegum when I was a kid, just after he joined the Air Force. He certainly didn't have to offer me any, but he always did. None of my friends would have done such a thing. I was convinced it meant he thought I was going to make a good brother in time, someone worthy of the U.S. Air Force and its fighter pilots.

Nadine was standing in the middle of the kitchen with a dustpan in her hand. The clock on the stove said 2:37. She put her arm around Jocko and gave him a soft peck on his good cheek. "Does it hurt?" she asked.

"Not a bit. Can't feel a thing," Jocko said. "Old Mike fixed me up."

I said my goodbyes and started to leave. Nadine followed me to the door and we hugged and kissed goodbye in the dark alcove, but my heart wasn't in it. She told me to be sure to call her tomorrow and I said I would. I walked out to my VW, and she stood at the door and watched me until I had gotten in and slammed the door, started the engine, and pulled away.

The streets were almost deserted, and the full moon was out and everything seemed amazingly bright and clear. I drove hurriedly back across town through the dazzling, empty streets to my parents' quiet house, tiptoed to my room, undressing like a shadow, and fell into bed as soon as I got there.

When Jocko came back from the Air Force in 1953—ten years before—he was twenty-five and I was eleven. My parents and I were living in a maroon-shingled ranch on a lush half-acre in another suburb of Cincinnati and my father was the manager of a radio station, and Dad told Jocko he could live with us until he could put down some roots and get a job and start making it on his own.

At twenty-five, Jocko was a quiet, well-built young man, about five-seven, with short, slicked-back hair and an aura of sensitivity and refinement and suppressed anguish not unlike the actor James Dean. My father always claimed, often in Jocko's presence like an apology, that Jocko was smaller than he should have been because, as a child, he had had double pneumonia and almost died. Jocko was the smallest offspring in a family whose male members took more than usual macho pride in feats of strength and physical prowess; and in the Air Force he had been a drill instructor and, later, a military policeman, roles that he must have chosen to prove something, not because he was especially well suited by temperament to perform them. He was certainly tough enough to have done so, but so laid back that, even now, I have a hard time imagining how he must have managed it. Unless he had been drinking, he was a man who seldom raised his voice. How could he have yelled at fresh recruits and humiliated them and called them names?

Jocko had been away for a long time, and while we were growing up he was so much older than I was that we had never really gotten to know one another. My only other sibling had died as a baby, so I had grown up as an only child with an only child's self-possession and sense of loneliness. I didn't have a clue about what Jocko might have felt about me.

But I certainly knew what I felt about him. I was just a kid and he was already a man—I thought he was the equivalent of a movie star or a dignified visitor from outer space. I thought it was nifty almost beyond belief to have such a person actually sleep in the other twin bed in my room and be my brother. I would wake up early in the morning and there he would be, snoring away in the other bed, and I would get up and creep quietly over there and gaze at his sleeping face, which seemed so peaceful and heroic, and his muscular arm resting across the pillow, and the broad palm of his hand, and the pulse beating in his wrist. Then I would carefully examine the items lying on top of the dresser—his big wristwatch, his wallet, a set of car keys with a plastic Mercury fob, a pack of matches, a pair of aviator sunglasses, an Ace comb—and try to comprehend his unfathomable life in outposts around the world.

As I say, Jocko was my half-brother, and that made him seem even more mysterious. What *was* a half-brother? I couldn't figure it out. I knew a lot of embarrassing things had happened before I was born: the war, World War II, during which my father was badly wounded—he had had terrible nightmares and sometimes drank too much in those days—my parents' itinerant life, moving every year to some new house in some new neighborhood while my father worked for some new company, trying to get rich—we were still doing that even after I was born. I could comprehend those things, if somewhat feebly at first.

But the idea that my father had been married to someone else before he had met my mother, someone named Lucille whose name was never mentioned in our house, though she was sometimes referred to obliquely as "Jocko's mother"—that idea seemed extremely improbable, seemed almost inconceivable to me.

Judging from his attitude, my father must have felt it was a personal failure he had to atone for, to struggle to live down. He did this by trying to be a model father and husband and bread-winner, by doting on my mother and me, by making up to me in every possible way for what he had failed to provide for little Jocko.

About 4:30 in the morning the phone rang and it was Jocko on the other end. He sounded a whole lot drunker than when I had left him a couple of hours earlier. He said he was leaving town once and for all, and if I ever wanted to see him again, he was at an all-night diner on Red Bank Road. Did I know the place? I said I thought I could find it. If I was coming, he said, I'd better get there in a hurry because he wasn't staying there long. He had to hit the road. He said even if I made it there before he left, it would probably be the last time I would ever see him because he was never going back to that house with Gloria in it—not if his life depended on it—and he was never going back to that goddamned used car lot, and he was never coming back to this lousy city with its lousy losing baseball team, period.

I said I would get dressed and be there as quickly as I could—I would gladly break the speed limit—but I wanted him to promise to wait for me because I wanted to talk to him before he left. He said he might be able to wait for twenty minutes but he doubted if he could wait any longer than that—he had to be somewhere. I asked him where that might be, where I could reach him, but he mumbled something I couldn't hear and hung up.

I got dressed at lightning speed and tore out to the garage and squealed out the driveway. It was still dark and humid outside. I rolled down the window of my VW and leaned against the door and drove like Mario Andretti, as if my life depended on it, burning up the road as if I had never heard that traffic laws existed. If they tried to pull me over, I would simply tell them the truth: it was a family emergency. As far as I could tell, it was a matter of life and death.

Within a few weeks after Jocko got out of the Air Force in 1953, my father gave him a job at the radio station selling sixty-second spots—his salary based largely on commissions. Even though such work was not at all natural for Jocko, I suppose he had an inclination to do what my father encouraged him to do. But, before too long, it became evident to everyone that Jocko just didn't have it in him to succeed at this kind of sales work. He wasn't selling anything, and he hated it.

It was along about this time that Jocko met Rose. Rose was working as a roller-skating car-hop at a Frische's Big Boy, and one day Jocko pulled in for lunch in his big blue Mercury and Rose skated up to his window and into his life. She was a bleached blonde, a Catholic girl with an angel's sweet face, great legs, and a heart-shaped birthmark on her right shoulder. She knew how to talk to little brothers without a hint of condescension and without hiding a certain natural feminine admiration for the male of the species. Up to that time, aside from my mother, I thought she was by far the most interesting woman I had ever actually talked to.

Jocko married Rose, his first wife, in nineteen fifty-six, and after casting around for a few months to find work, he decided to take out a big loan and buy into a Sunoco franchise and run his own filling station. The work was menial, but the idea of pure independence must have appealed to him. He could open when he wanted, close up when he felt like it. He didn't have to sell anybody anything—they would come to him. He would wash every driver's windshield and make the station a model of friendliness and good service, and he didn't have to follow anybody's orders except his own. He felt he had been taking orders long enough—from both my father and the Air Force.

He figured that after he made a little money and paid off his loan he could hire some high-school kids to man the place and start looking for other investments. He found a station in Middletown, Ohio, about thirty miles north of Cincinnati, and with my father's help he bought a house within a block of the station and told Rose she could retire from car-hopping.

A parallel scheme he had for making money was to raise purebred Chihuahuas on the side. He bought four of them, two males and two females, and started breeding them in a little shed in his backyard, and before long, one of the bitches had puppies and Jocko had ten little dogs running around in his backyard, yapping up a storm at anyone who came within earshot.

Jocko would take off for the station early in the morning and knock himself out pumping gas and wiping windshields, and Rose would lie around the house watching soap operas and game shows and doing house-work and cooking and tending to the dogs. At noon she would take Jocko a sack lunch and sit around the station for a while, sharing sandwiches and smoking cigarettes. Then she would head back to the house and try to find some way to kill the afternoon before it was time to start dinner.

They intended to have babies of their own—Rose, especially, was eager to start a family—but month after month went by and Rose couldn't get pregnant. Within a year the dogs had another litter, and they sold a few of the pups from the first batch but still had thirteen dogs; and Rose started making sarcastic jokes about how the dogs could get pregnant whenever they wanted to but the people who lived there couldn't, for some reason.

Jocko kept three of the dogs in the house by then, and Jocko and Rose both made over them constantly. Whenever we arrived for a visit Jocko would make his favorite little dog, Princess, show off all the new tricks he had taught her since the last time we had visited. Without a doubt, that Princess was a smart little Chihuahua.

By the end of his third year with Sunoco, it was plain that the station was not going to make Jocko into a millionaire any time soon. The locals had more or less deserted it because it was out of the way and had been through a series of owners. Though Jocko was handy with tools he was not really a mechanic, so there was very little to be made on anything more complicated than an occasional oil change.

In addition, the dogs were costing more to raise than they were bringing in. The truth was that Jocko became so attached to the dogs that he didn't want to part with any of them, and he would ask unreasonable prices for them and deliberately jinx a sale whenever potential buyers would come around to look.

He and Rose had several fights over "the dog problem," as Rose started to call it. The dogs were getting on her nerves. She got so mad during one such argument with Jocko that she threatened to go back to car-hopping to bring in more money and get out of the house and away from the dogs once in a while, and Jocko said he didn't give a damn if she did.

So Rose went back to car-hopping, and Jocko started to feel like a failure again, in spite of his best efforts. It nearly drove him crazy to think of Rosie skating around the drive-in in one of those incredible short skirts that was hardly more than a pair of sheer panties with a cloth border around it and flirting with every Tom, Dick, or Harry who drove up and gave her the eye, just to make an extra quarter tip—even if her disposition did seem to improve at first. He spent a lot of time sitting in his greasy-armed desk chair between gas customers imagining what Rose might be doing and wishing it could be like the old days when she would bring him his lunch and sit across the desk laughing and eating cookies and drawing seductively on her Viceroys.

Then one day he came home from the station and Rose wasn't there. She didn't get home until about ten that night, and then when she burst in she was carrying a pizza and acting far too jovial and sweet and making some flimsy excuse about working a couple hours of overtime because they were so busy at the drive-in.

His mother had deserted him when he was ten. Now Rose was doing the same thing. He must have felt that there was something about him personally that was missing, that simply couldn't hold them.

He hired a detective who came back after the first week and said he had followed Rose to a motel three times that week, where she was shacking up with some traveling salesman from Indianapolis.

He had pictures of them going into the motel together, but in order to make it a clean, uncontested divorce they would have to catch them at the motel together "in the act" and get pictures and serve her with the papers. Jocko could see it for himself and serve as a witness. Looking at those snapshots, Jocko was so overcome with anguish, with a tightness in his throat, that he gave the go-ahead.

Within a few days, the detective called back from the Sunnyside Motel, and Jocko jumped in his Jeep and buzzed on over. The detective was waiting in the office, where he had the warrant and had alerted the proprietor. They walked right down the little sidewalk in front of the units, and the detective quietly unlocked the lock to number twenty-three and threw open the door and started gunning away with his flash camera.

Sure enough, there was Rose in bed with some creep; Rose, his own true love, screaming and crying and acting injured, and the detective served her with the papers, and Jocko walked away and got in his Jeep and sped down to a local bar and drank cheap scotch until he passed out.

After that, Jocko lost the Sunoco station and declared bankruptcy, sold the house, and got rid of all his dogs. He came back to live with us for a while and moved back into my room. Sometimes at night he would babble and whimper in his sleep, and I felt so sorry for him, but I didn't know what I could do. He was a grown man and I was just a teenager.

Except for the Air Force, it seemed he had failed at everything he had ever tried, and I, on the other hand, seemed destined to succeed but be embarrassed by his presence merely because of my good fortune. My very existence seemed a constant reminder to him of all that had been denied him. He had flunked out of school; I was always a good student, a good boy—I couldn't have been otherwise. Worse yet, at that time, I was having a growth spurt. I was six feet tall and still growing. I was good at baseball, basketball, and track, and brought home trophies and ribbons and district championships and all-star jacket-patches that dad was so proud of he could never stop rhapsodizing. What Jocko had had to suffer was simply not fair. I didn't blame him for any of it—none of us did.

• • •

When I located the diner on Red Bank Road, a thin film of daylight was just sliding across its aluminum and plate-glass walls and brightening the concrete pavement and the abutment of the distant viaduct. I quickly scanned the cars in the lot as I pulled in, hoping to see Jocko's Gran Prix. I didn't see it, but I hurried inside, fearing I had missed him, and found him sitting at the counter, sipping a cup of coffee. He turned to look at me, then turned back to his coffee without changing expression. His hair was uncombed and he was still wearing the same bloody shirt under his jacket and he still had the three Band-Aids stuck to his chin. His eyes were two bloodshot slits. I sat down on the stool next to him and ordered coffee.

"You don't look so hot," I said.

"You wouldn't either, brother . . ."

"You and Gloria have another fight?"

"I don't even want to think about it. I'm never going to see her again, so it doesn't really matter, does it?"

"Why wouldn't you see her? Maybe this is just a bad night. Maybe you'll feel differently about it in the morning."

"No, I won't. It *is* morning. See out there—it's almost morning already."

"I mean *tomorrow* morning. You haven't had any sleep. You're not thinking straight. Why don't you come home with me and sleep it off—then maybe you'll feel better about everything."

"Naw—I've got to *be* somewhere. It's time for a change, and this time I'm going to go through with it."

"Where do you have to be?"

"Somewhere . . . I can't tell you." Here we go again, I thought.

The waitress poured my coffee and pushed a small ceramic creamer after it. I poured cream in my coffee and brought the hot mug to my lips and blew on it and put it back down.

"Maybe I'd like to be part of it."

"Naw—you wouldn't."

"How do you know without asking me? I might. We could be in on it together."

"I just don't think you would. It's not your kind of situation."

"What the hell does that mean?" I blew on the coffee again and took a sip. I wasn't sure whether this was just drunk-talk or something serious.

"This is something I just have to do alone—that's all."

"Sure."

"I think you should stay out of it," he said.

"If I should stay out of it, maybe you should stay out of it." He shook his head and sighed.

"The way I look at it is this—what have I got to lose? I'm never going to see Gloria again, anyway. I'm never going back to that brick house. I mean—why should I? I'm never going to . . ." He put a hand up over his eyes and bowed his head. We were both embarrassed and silent for a moment. I wanted desperately to say the right thing, something to help.

"Why don't you come back to school with me?" I said. "You could stay there until you decide what to do. I've got plenty of extra room in my apartment."

"In Yellow Springs?"

"Sure. It's a nice town. You'd like it there. You could just take it easy for a while and get your bearings."

"What in the hell would I do there?"

"Hang around with me. You could find a job if you wanted to. We'd have a great time."

"Hang around with a bunch of college kids—sure."

"Hey, it's a big little-town. You could make your own friends. We could hang around. You could stay at my place as long as you wanted to, until you could meet some new people. There are a lot of people there. Then go off with your own friends—call up once in a while to say hello. It's an easy place to live. You'd like it. Eventually, you could get your own place, and I could come over for a beer."

"I don't think so." He tamped his cellophaned pack of Chesterfields on the edge of the counter and held the pack up to his lips and pulled out one weed and lighted up. He showed the pack to me and I shook my head.

"This other thing doesn't sound like such a great deal to me," I said.

"What do you know about it? You don't even know what it is." He blew a thin stream of smoke up over our heads.

"I just don't think you're the kind of guy who would get involved in something like this. I'm surprised to hear about it."

"Maybe I am. Maybe you were wrong about me all along."

"I don't think so," I said. "We wouldn't even have to tell anybody about this, you know. You could just come up there with me, and we could keep it confidential. Gloria wouldn't know where you were, and we wouldn't tell Dad, either. Then, later, you could call him if you wanted to. Or maybe you'd decide not to."

He dragged heavily on his cigarette again and exhaled. "Maybe you're right. Maybe that's not such a bad idea."

"It's a damned good idea." I got out a ballpoint and started drawing a map on the napkin. I drew a schematic of the streets of Yellow Springs, Ohio, and labelled them, and then I showed him where my apartment was, right near the middle with an X. "It's only a couple of hours on the road. Just head out like you're going to Middletown."

"What are you doing here, Mike? I mean, why do you really *care* what I do or not?"

"Because I'm your brother, that's why." Jocko looked at the napkin and thought it over. "Right there is where I live," I said, pointing at the X. "It's easy to find. The key is under the mat."

"I'll find it," he said, crushing out his Chesterfield butt. "That is, provided I decide to go up there. It's in the same direction that I was going anyway." He folded up the napkin and put it in his pocket.

"So what are you going to do?" I said.

"I'll think about it on the way," he said. "I'll start out and I'll decide when I get to the turn-off."

"I just wish you'd decide ahead of time," I said. "If I knew you were going up there, I'd go back and get my stuff now and meet you. I could be up there this afternoon and help you get moved in."

"Hey—I really ought to get going now, you know." He stood up from the stool and laid two dollars on the counter next to his cup and saucer.

We walked out of the diner together and stood for a moment on the front walk, where traffic hummed from the distant viaduct. "Give me a call, will you, if you decide not to come," I said. "That way I'll know."

"Sure," he said. "I could do that. I'll think it over and then I'll give you a call." I knew by the way he said it that he probably wouldn't.

"Good," I said. We shook hands. "I hope you decide to come."

"So long, Mike." He patted me on the shoulder.

"So long, Jock." He was only thirty-five, but he seemed so worn out and his face was so lined and haggard in the eerie morning brightness that the cuts were more visible—he could have been sixty. His light eyes seemed bruised but intense as he squinted at me, friendly but opaque, altogether impenetrable, as always. I watched him walk around the side of the diner and get in his car, a small, dignified man, surprisingly handsome. "Don't forget," I called, "the key is under the mat."

He gave a somewhat nautical little wave, almost a salute, and got in his car and started off.

I got in my VW and drove back to my parents' house across town. They weren't awake yet; it was only 6 A.M. I lay down on the bed in my room and fell asleep myself. When I woke up, it was already noon and the sun was beating down on the windowsill and bedspread and across my face. I felt disoriented and weak and wasn't sure for a minute where I was. Then I jumped up with a start, realizing how late it was, and started throwing my things into my suitcase and getting ready to take off for Yellow Springs to meet Jocko.

I drove straight through with only a gas stop. When I got near Fairborn, I passed an accident where someone had run off the road and flipped over and mashed the roof of a red Chevrolet, and a wrecker was up ahead with another car. I had a bad moment when I was certain the car bouncing along on the hoist chain would be Jocko's Pontiac. But it wasn't a Pontiac; it was an old beat-up pickup truck.

I kept thinking about that morning in the diner. I never should have let him go off on his own. I was afraid it was a mistake at the time, but I didn't know what else to do. I should have made him come with me— then and there—but I knew, even as I had the thought, that he never would have come.

I drove on into Yellow Springs and parked in my space beside the apartment building where I lived and went up to my rooms. There was no note on the door, and the key was undisturbed under the mat. Inside, there was no sign that anyone had been there—it was just as I had left it. I made myself a snack and sat there at my kitchen table munching on a sandwich and drinking a glass of milk and staring out the window into the street below.

After a while, it started to get dark, and the streetlights came on. Once I thought I saw Jocko's Pontiac make a slow pass in front of the building, but the car didn't turn around, so I guessed my eyes were playing tricks on me. I was tired, and I figured Jocko wasn't going to show up, and it disappointed me. I wanted a chance to help him out, and now it looked as if I'd missed that chance.

I remembered that I had forgotten to call Nadine. I got her number out of my wallet and dialed it and let it ring twelve times, but no one answered. I dialed it again and let it ring twenty-five times. After that, I must have dozed off.

Along about ten, there was a loud knocking at my door, and I woke up with a start. I couldn't imagine who it might be at this hour. My mind was numb and full of mixed-up dreams. I shambled toward the door and opened it, and damned if it wasn't Jocko, grinning from ear to ear. There was a woman standing there with him out in the hall, her arm draped around his neck like a wounded soldier.

"Hiya, Mike-o," he said, grabbing me by the shoulder. "Look what this old cat drug in!"

I was so groggy it took me a moment to realize that Jocko's new girlfriend was Nadine. In the light, she looked amazingly dissipated and angelic. She lurched toward me and reached up and planted a kiss on my startled face.

Atomic Love

Several dense areas requiring coned down compression views—please come in for FU mammogram ASAP.

Now, in the ladies room at LaGuardia Airport, Emily looks in the mirror and sees a strange woman—herself. Her eyes stare back with the rapt luminosity of the rabbits in the cosmetics experiments.

She is elegant, feminine in the dress; her body is muscular, sensuous, trim. She is *not* ill, not ill so far as anyone knows. She is colorful, alive, so healthy she is almost freakish, "radioactive" only in some Diane Arbus sort of way—peach-colored skin, red lips, bright eyes. Small laugh-lines on her nose and at the corners of her eyes—but those are hardly visible.

She is getting older—she is aging. But she doesn't look "old" yet—no, certainly not as old as she is—forty-two—still a beautiful woman, looking probably a lot closer to her "biological age" as determined last year by a series of tests at the health center. Because of her blood pressure and her heartbeat and her good habits, she is, biologically, twenty-nine. She takes out a thin gold compact and dusts her nose, then collects her bags and hurries on out into the lobby and through the crowd and down the escalator to the lower level.

When Emily was seven, they moved to Lost Vegas, and one day in school her teacher told the children they were going outside for a big surprise. They lined up on a high slope in front of the rows of schoolroom windows, swing-sets across the playground creaking in the breeze on a bright, clear morning, the sky, a perfect dome of blue above them. The children oohed and ahhed as they were treated to a spectacular event: an atomic cloud sprouting above the desert. She remembers it very clearly— it really happened.

Just this spring, thirty-five years later, Emily has received a letter from one of her long-lost classmates who is suing the Government, claiming that more than half of those children exposed to the testing following WW II—over half—have contracted cancer or some form of debilitating illness. Then she received the note from the hospital about returning for a follow-up X-ray. That was the thing that was just too upsetting to be believed. She knew she would do it. Of course, she would go in and have it done. But she knew, in advance, that they were simply mistaken. She was basically healthy. She wasn't worried.

Sometimes she feels amazingly inexperienced for a woman of her age, a blank slate, as if she were still twenty-nine, or even nineteen or seven. Truthfully, she doesn't feel any different on the inside than she did when she was nineteen; only the outside has changed, has ripened. The truth is she is an "older" woman but has had only one bona fide "affair"— so brief, unsuccessful, and so long ago that it hardly mattered. The word itself sounded ridiculous and totally unsuited to the situation, but what else should she call it? She doubts she is going to start another one now, in any case. That wasn't what this was all about, surely. But what if it was? If it was, so what?

They had met, she and Tom, quite accidentally, last June at a tennis resort in Vermont. They had corresponded regularly since. Now they were traveling their separate ways to Manhattan, supposedly on busi-ness, but actually to see each other—she, from southwestern Ohio; he, from Pennsylvania. The fact of the matter was that he was one of the most unusual men she had ever run into—he cared about her in some special way that gave her a new feeling about herself, and . . . she does have a legitimate reason for traveling to New York. She wants to decide about a line of imported baskets for the small greenhouse and nursery business she started running last spring.

A wave of heat buffeted Emily's face, and the bones inside her fingers seemed to shimmer in the blinding light. "Hide your eyes," the teacher called. For weeks, the clouds appeared, and whenever they went out for recess, small particles fell out of the air and dotted the playground.

A skycap intersects her path, says "M'am," and with her consent hoists her bags away, brushing close to her shoulder as he walks her toward the taxi area. "Ohhh," the black man says, "she looks like a jewel and she smells like a flau-wah." He must think she is from the South. He smiles into her face with harmless appreciation, showing a mouth full of beautiful teeth. "You know what I love?" he says, putting her luggage down on the pavement by the taxis. "You know what I love?" he says, bringing his droll face up to her. "Milk and honey." He hesitates, then rolls his eyes as if in an ecstasy of sensual satisfaction. "Milk stands for love. Milk is the *symbol* for love. And honey—why, honey is the best thing you've ever had. You're not married, are you?"

She nods her head.

"Ahh," he says, feigning disappointment. "Where you from?"

"Cincinnati."

"Where you stayin'? Maybe I'll call you later."

She shakes her head.

"No? Don't want me to call you later? Ahhh."

She smiles sympathetically. He isn't dangerous, just full of talk.

"Well, you have a good time now."

She gets in the yellow cab, and the skycap backs up and closes the door and waves, as the cab zooms away.

It isn't that George, her husband, is neglecting her on purpose, but that medicine is, as some of the doctors' wives often complain, a very jealous mistress. And this month he is away for two weeks, attending a medical convention in Belgium. And she was not invited. He is a good man, a successful man, but so involved in his career that he sometimes seems like a distant relative, a kindly paternal figure who visits home every week or so to check on her, as if she were yet another patient, or who falls into bed past midnight on any given night and instantly begins snoring. He is always so tired, so harried, his forehead creased with the weight of responsibility.

Tom's wife, on the other hand, seemed perfectly attentive, in the glimpses Emily had had of her at the resort. She was a striking woman with a pert curve of ash-blond hair (and a knack for looking good in a bathing suit) who reminded Emily of a sorority sister she had despised in college, a girl who had had too many boyfriends and too much social finesse and a complicated love-life. Tom had not mentioned her at all, except to say that he was, of course, married to her and committed to his children, two little boys—two little boys who Emily imagines, under different circumstances, might be her own. So far she and George have not been so lucky.

Until recently, Emily suspected her barrenness was George's fault. Then she began to wonder seriously about what the Bomb might have done to her. There had been so many tests that year, they had stopped paying attention. The bizarre events across the horizon were just another feature of Las Vegas in her memory—all-might-now-be-Lost-Vegas. One of the accounts she had read about the atomic testing claimed that at a distance of 360 miles from ground zero—a lot farther away than she had been—rabbits were discovered whose eyes had been scorched, and the retinal burns were the exact shapes of tiny mushroom clouds.

The cab rockets across the bridge over the East River, and she tries to adjust her feelings to the monstrosity of the city, the dingy buildings in all directions, the contorted, teeming fury of the place, the forbidding maze of girders and stone, cars careening wildly beside her, the magnificent skyline rising promisingly, ominously, above her, like a vision or a nightmare.

She checks in at the Plaza, showers and changes, and is working on her hair with the blow-dryer when the phone rings. Tom is here now too—he made it—his voice so rich and masculine, so full of caring for her. She rushes down to meet him in the lobby, and she can watch herself in the lavish mirrors as she moves down the hall toward him, the sweep of expensive carpet, the darkly wooded wainscoting, chandeliers glistening above her head—such a strange, healthy, good-looking woman. Is it anyone she knows? Tom is suddenly there, smiling, coming toward her, and she can see it in his eyes, too—such a good-looking woman—as they move together and embrace.

He hadn't changed much since Vermont, his straight, elegant nose, his handsome jawline and chin, his light, penetrating eyes, gazing now off into the distance—even the back of his neck is attractive. He is such an exciting man, such a masculine man, she is proud to be with him. She knows from experience it would be possible to nibble on his earlobes if she stands on her tiptoes. To her mind, these seem just about the ideal proportions. Not that she has had much opportunity to try it—only the last night at the resort when they had lingered in the darkened lodge to say goodbye, and he had held her for a moment or two longer than discretion permitted.

"How have you been, Emily?"

"Looking forward to seeing you, looking forward to this moment—this exact moment."

He sighs. "I can't believe we're actually doing it."

"I can't believe it either," Emily says. "I can't believe I had the guts."

"I can't believe I had the luck." They both laugh. Tom squeezes her to him and kisses her lightly on the shoulder.

At dinner, she finds a way to tell him about her marriage, about her loneliness, obliquely rather than directly, but he seems to understand; he listens with a wonderful calm and sympathy. What she wants to ask him but does not have the courage is: How often should a man make love to a woman who is his wife? Is there any unwritten code on this subject that men are supposed to know something about? What should a wife's response be if the time stretches from a week to a month to three months? Does three months mean they have tacitly agreed on a permanent state of celibacy? Does three months mean the marriage is dissolved? Does it mean he is not a good husband? Would it be revealing too much to ask Tom those sorts of questions?

"One thing I know for sure," Emily says over drinks, "I can't—there's no way that I could ever let myself start."

"Start what?" Tom says, munching on his ice.

"An affair with you." She feels she must be blunt, but saying the stupid word embarrasses her. She feels her cheeks getting hot, her ears burning beneath her hair. She hopes no one seated nearby in the velvet-and-mahogany dimness can overhear this little conversation, even if they are strangers.

"What about a friendship?" His eyes study her face.

"That's what I'm really looking for, I think. A friendship."

"That's what this is, if you ask me. I can handle that."

You liar, she thinks. "But can I, that's the question?" He seems so perfectly, maddeningly, calm about all of this.

"What if you just pretended that I was some kind of sexual surrogate prescribed to help you improve your marriage?" His face cracks into laugh-lines and his lips curl into a droll pucker.

"See what I mean! You're a bad influence." She laughs in spite of herself, but she begins to worry if she hasn't revealed too much.

"Just an idea. We wouldn't let it interfere with our friendship—I promise."

"You're terrible. You're not serious at all."

"Whatever you want, Emily, really." Maybe he is serious, after all.

"Stop being so cooperative."

"In ten years, I think you'll regret it, that's all. I know I will."

Her face, she knows, shows a stricken look—she agrees. If only she weren't so transparent, such a hopeless and defenseless sitting duck.

Following the meal, they linger over the drinks.

"I wanted to tell you," Emily whispers, still uneasy that someone might overhear, "that I keep having these . . . waves of pain . . . when I think about you or look at you. These waves of pain just keep washing over me, and I don't know what to do about it. I thought maybe if I talked about it, it would help."

"It might," he says.

"Why do I feel this way then?"

"Why do you think?"

"I don't know—because I want you and I can't have you?" she says.

"But you can have me. That's why I'm here."

"Because I know I won't be able to deal with the consequences?"

"So you just turn around and go home—and avoid it?"

"No, I do what I came here to do—the business I came here for, without the complications."

"Okay," he says.

"Don't you see—that would be so much easier and safer. I could just go on doing what I have been. I can just be myself."

"Then that's what you should do, Emily."

"You think so?"

"No doubt at all."

"That would really be okay with you?"

"I'd support it one hundred percent."

The waiter appears with the bill, and Tom reaches for his wallet and places an American Express platinum card in the small tray. They finish their drinks.

Out on the street, dusk is settling and the lights seem brighter, more dazzling. They walk in silence for a while.

"Well, I feel *better* after our conversation. Oh, what a relief. It helped me to talk about it."

"I'm glad it helped *you*," he says.

"Oh no—it didn't help you?" He rolls his eyes at her like an animal in the throes of some visceral agony. "Oh, my god," she says. "I'm sorry." It had never occurred to her that *he* might need helping.

They walk straight from the restaurant back to the hotel, and up to his room to say goodnight. Suddenly, she feels worse than ever. Now she has really ruined it. He seems quiet, brooding, but not reproachful, simply resigned and disappointed. "Now what?" he says, staring out the huge window at the lights of the buildings across Fifth Avenue and into the chasm of the street below, full of blurred, silent traffic.

She moves up behind him, meaning to stand there and stare out at the night and at their reflection in the dark glass, but without thinking about it, without a thought in her mind, her elbows rise up over her head and her hands unfasten the snap of her dress, unzip it quickly to the small of her back, and begin feebly to unbutton the pearl buttons of his shirt, her hands shaking miserably, as if they have nearly lost the ability to function.

Of course, making love to him changes everything.

Afterwards, while they are lying there, the phone rings. Emily jumps.

"Who could that be?" she says.

"It's probably my wife," Tom says.

"Are you going to answer it?"

"I should," he says.

"I'll go into the other room," she says, getting up quickly and hiding in the bathroom.

"Oh, hello, Sweetheart," she hears him say through the closed door. "No, I just walked in. I'm glad you caught me. It's been a busy day here." She doesn't want to hear another word. She plugs her ears with her fingers, then stuffs Kleenex in to blank out every sound, watching herself in the mirror as she cocks her head and forces the wads of tissue in as tightly as possible, her lovely, flushed face, with its rabbit eyes, as expressionless as a stone.

But in the morning she feels better.

They walk hand in hand down Fifth Avenue to an outdoor cafe by the Stanhope Hotel, across the street from the Metropolitan Museum. All the while, Emily's mind is filling with fields of desire for him. Tom. She repeats his name over and over in her mind.

"What are you thinking about?" he asks her as they choose two seats in the front of the cafe.

"You don't want to know," she says.

"Yes, yes, I do want to know—tell me."

"Well . . . I was just thinking about you," Emily confesses. Tom's blue eyes sparkle when he smiles.

"I don't mind at all," he says, reaching over to kiss her.

On their table is a bouquet of tea roses in a lovely fluted vase. The waiter comes, and they study the menus, the sunlight falling through the glass canopy above and across the page, burnishing the raised lettering as if each item has special importance. *Enjoy this moment,* Emily tells herself.

"I go to a dance-exercise class. Good workout. I always do some kind of exercise," Emily says.

"Swimming and tennis, and what else?"

"A few years ago, I took karate. Took it for two years and earned my second belt. Does that make you afraid?"

"Not a bit."

"I can break boards with my feet. What about that—does that make you afraid?"

"You'd like to have something that makes me afraid?" Tom says.

"Yes."

"There are some things about you that frighten me, Emily, but they are not your feet."

"Ohh, you."

"Besides, I may not be able to break boards with my feet, but if I get into trouble with you, I can probably outrun you."

"Don't count on it," Emily says.

"Why don't we go back to the Plaza and you can show me the tricks you do with your feet. I bet you have several tricks I haven't seen yet."

"That's exactly the kind of remark that could land you in big trouble, buster." Emily reaches out and punches him lightly on the arm.

"Watch it," he says. "I'm completely defenseless."

"You're asking for it."

"Keep those feet under the table at all times."

Across the street from the hotel is Central Park, and they can see a row of carriages lined up waiting to take people for rides inside the gates. "You want to do that?" Tom says. "It might be fun."

"Sure, I'd like it. I've always wanted to try something like that," Emily says. But George would never want to "waste time" on something so frivolous, she thinks. They hurry across the street and wait in line. Up close, their carriage is disappointingly shabby, and the poor horse is so tired-looking and hot. Emily wonders if he is abused by the driver, a man who looks like a gypsy or an ancient circus barker in a top hat and a tattered, ridiculous tux and tails. He is unshaven and seems, in some essential way, disreputable.

But once underway there is, after all, a kind of magic—to the steady clopping of the horse's hooves on the pavement, the sway of his rump, the slow-paced promenade beneath overhanging branches heavy with the summer ripeness of leaves. She hadn't realized how beautiful it would be here in late July—warm and humid, of course, but so pleasant, after all. She knows she will remember this buggy ride with a powerful sense of nostalgia and wistfulness when she returns to Ohio, and she wants to engrave every detail in her memory. Tom touches her arm and points something out to her, a squirrel or a rock, she isn't sure. Emily stares for a moment in the direction he is indicating and then shifts her awkward position in the seat and slips her shoes off and curls up against him.

The breeze billows up under her dress. Tom is holding her and kissing her and she doesn't know why she does it—she is completely astonished at herself—but she slowly slips off her panties—staring blatantly into his eyes as she is doing it, and tucks them into her purse. Suddenly he is pressing himself into her and she is letting him, urging him, in fact, whispering things into his ear that she has never said to anyone before in her life, as he squeezes her harder and harder against the leather seat of the carriage, and the carriage rattles slowly along in a dream. Some small distant part of her wants to feel embarrassed, wants to worry itself with whether the driver will turn around or someone walking in the park will see what they are doing. But that part is out-voted and overwhelmed by what they are presently doing so nicely, so beautifully and muscularly, together, like an Olympic feat. The way it wells up inside her like madness, like a terrible thirst, then radiates through her body in wave after wave of pleasure is such a surprise. Such a luxury it seems, to be making love in the middle of the day, forgetting everything, abandoning everything.

Tom is talking about how he had once considered med-school himself—what a coincidence. Well, he had taken a few courses—he had gone that far. If he had studied medicine, maybe they would have met sooner, Emily thinks, and she would never have married someone else. Tom might be living in Cincinnati with its great medical facilities instead of Pittsburgh, and she could see him every day—even if they weren't married yet. This eerie alternate life suddenly seems to Emily far preferable to her own. But, instead, Tom had studied history and philosophy and gone on to Law School and a life in Pittsburgh. Too bad. He didn't like the smell of the chemistry lab. He didn't care for the horrors of zoology, the reek of formaldehyde, the obsession with dead things. The law seemed so much cleaner and more civilized, he said. Too bad, she thinks. People just don't realize how one small decision, perhaps entirely whimsical or accidental, can change everything.

"You made the right decision," Emily says. "Medicine is so heartless and demanding. Doctors have to be saints. It isn't worth it."

"And what about their wives?" Tom says.

"Their wives! Their wives have to try to be saints, too," Emily says, "but some of them never make it."

"Emily, sweetheart, you're not cut out for sainthood. Who needs it? Sainthood means depriving yourself; it means mortification of the flesh. You're too earthy for that."

"You don't think I would qualify for sainthood?"

"You're much better as an angel, I would say, than a saint." Tom pats her hand sweetly.

Emily feels herself smiling at this, glowing all over, in spite of herself. She should feel guilty, but he won't let her. What should she feel guilty about, exactly? At this moment she cannot resurrect a single particle of guilt, and maybe that in itself—this utter and complete absence of conscience—is what she really ought to feel most guilty about.

• • •

Back home after her trip, she walks around the deserted house in a daze. She wanders out to the greenhouse and turns on the sprinklers, her hands moving swiftly, automatically, to cradle and prod, to pluck at dead leaves here and there—her beautiful plants—her mind unfocusing like the mist of warm water filling the ripe, pungent air. A terrible sense of longing and loneliness fills her, and she feels suddenly on the verge of tears. She and the plants are exactly as fecund and helpless as one another, exactly as beautiful and useless.

If Tom could only be here to see the greenhouse, to see her life, it would be so satisfying to her. He said he loved her, but how could he? He didn't really know her yet. She wanted him to know so much more, everything there was to know. If he were only here, they would have such a good time. . . .

She imagines the two of them sitting on a picnic blanket in a meadow, far from any intruders. They are sipping wine, and she is wearing a white lace dress and exquisite lingerie and a wide-brimmed sun hat like something out of the nineteenth century. She reaches for his hand, and he turns toward her, smiling into her eyes, and begins to unbutton her bodice and slowly to kiss her shoulders. For some reason, this makes her feel tragically depressed. She sits down to caress herself, to lightly touch her shoulder, but the pleasant feeling is gone.

She wanders back into the house and—staring out the bay window at the deserted yard, the gray, overcast sky, the wind-swept emptiness—writes a confused, ambivalent letter, describing her condition as a kind of disease from which she must make every effort to recover.

"We need to talk to each other soon," she writes, "because I really don't understand what is happening. I keep wondering if when you see me again, you'll realize it was all in your mind. I'm reading *Love in the Western World* by Denis de Rougement, and each time I read a new chapter in it I distrust what I feel for you and what you feel for me."

Tom's response is to call her up and invite her to travel to New York to see him again from the twenty-third to the twenty-fifth of August. He says he knows he is in love with her—she can be sure of that—and that de Rougement is a waste of time, that she already knows more about love than de Rougement ever did. His voice is so smooth and masculine over the telephone, it gives her chills. She has to hug herself to calm down. After his phone call, she is so keyed up she puts on her new jogging outfit, tight fluorescent nylon, admiring herself at some length in her bedroom mirror, and then runs miles and miles out through the neighboring farmland, alternately worrying and gloating, cruising effortlessly along deserted country roads between lush meadows and the stares of puzzled cows.

Urgent that you call for appt ASAP. FU mammogram rec requiring coned down compression views of dense areas.

The day before Emily is scheduled to leave for New York, she feels so dizzy and hot in the greenhouse that she wanders back inside and searches in the cluttered medicine cabinet for the thermometer. She finds it and washes it off and shakes it out and almost breaks it accidentally against the porcelain throat of the lavatory, she is so disoriented.

"Damn it," she says at her flakey image in the mirror. She slides the cool glass between her lips, noticing the pinkness of her delicate pointed tongue, then licks the glass seductively to observe the effect. "Damn you," she says again, watching her eyes narrow into sharp slits.

Emily lies down on the nearby sofa and lays her hand across her own hot forehead for comfort. She *can't* get sick now, of all times! She won't let herself get sick. She has too much to do. She has to get ready, pack her bag, pick up the ticket from the travel agent, go to the store, go to the bank. All the plans are made—she *has* to see Tom and get everything settled this week. She can't go on without settling it now. She *will* see him tomorrow whether she is sick or not, so she might as well pretend to be healthy.

She pulls out the thermometer and glares at it in the light from the near window. Almost 102 degrees! She sinks back into the sofa cushions and almost breaks into tears. No—she will just have to find some way to tough it out! She will eat Excedrins like candy, if necessary, and take the hottest bath she can stand right now and scald the germs to death. She will get a good night's sleep and maybe she can knock it out overnight. If that doesn't work, it's probably a virus anyway—or breast cancer!—so there's nothing to be done in the short term. She might as well be sick in New York as be sick at home.

"The good news is that I'm here," she tells Tom when she greets him in the hotel lobby the next day. "The bad news is that I've caught some miserable bug and you'd better not kiss me or you might catch it."

"Oh, no," Tom says, hugging her to his fragrant lapels. "Are you miserable or what?"

"Semi-miserable and light-headed and very angry at myself, but glad to be here, anyway."

"Oh, you poor thing. We'll have to take it very easy and be careful with you. We'll have to treat you with kid gloves."

"I could get into that," she says, sounding to herself very much like some teen-aged movie star. "I could get *into* that," she says again. *Who am I?* she wonders, to say such a stupid thing.

Her body seems to be on fire, she is so hot, but her head is so woozy, can she actually enjoy it? She is so drowsy it is as if all this jerking and floundering on the lovely flowered bedspread is happening to someone else or in a dream or a movie. Tom is above her, now behind her, now whispering in her ear. She can see them in the mirror, and now he is kissing her feet. "Are these the dangerous parts?" he is saying. "They don't look so dangerous to me." She is a musical instrument, a blind cello moving through the lower registers, a giddy wind-up toy, a honky-tonk piano, a wailing and keening bagpipe, and there is nothing she can do to prevent it. But is it Emily he is making love to? Is it the real Emily or some sordid imitation Emily? Did he read a book on sexual techniques so that he would know all the right moves, all the right things to say to her? How else would he know them all so well? She means to ask him that as soon as she can form the words in her mouth, but since intelligent speech is not possible in her present condition, not possible over her moaning, she lets it burn in her memory, to save for some future moment, some other despondent interchange between them, when she will be clear-headed and calm and direct, and she will catch him off-guard and she will say, "Oh, Tom, please. Please, I . . . please!"

"Goodnight," Emily says.

"Goodnight," Tom says and starts to kiss her on the lips but, at the last instant, diverts the kiss to her ear. Mustn't catch her affliction. Doctor's orders.

The phone rings and Tom answers it.

"Hi, Sweetie," he says. Emily's heart wobbles in her chest. *Not this again!* She doesn't want to hear it. She leaps to her feet and flees into the bathroom, where she ignores everything but the need to get dressed and retreat to the privacy of her own room. She slips out, unseen, not wanting to hear any more of the lying and hypocrisy that streams from Tom's tongue and into the telephone lines with the ease of flowing water. How can he be so animated and casual about it with her still on the bed, still in the same room? She imagines the wires starting to sizzle and explode. She hates this situation. She hates him for doing this to her.

Her headache is brutal. Her message light is on, blinking a bright red. The front desk informs her that George called. Wonderful. She gets undressed and pulls back the covers and lies down. She is so upset she is afraid she will say something unforgivable when Tom calls. She checks her watch—it is 1:13. She is looking forward to giving him a piece of her mind. By 1:30, it becomes clear to her that Tom has probably gone to sleep. What a man—he loves her so much, he is so attached to her, that he doesn't even have the courtesy to call to say goodnight. Saying goodnight to his wife is sufficient. Is there a message in this that anyone but a fool could see? Emily puts the pillow over her head and presses it against her temples. What floats by in the blackness of her eye sockets is the retinal memory of Tom turning his face away, not wanting to kiss her. That, and the cadaverous face of the disreputable gypsy carriage driver in the park, smirking because he knows what she likes to do on carriage rides. Oh, God! What is she doing here, sick and miserable in a strange room so far from home?

At brunch Tom is wearing his glasses—his contacts were hurting his eyes—and he doesn't look like himself. The glasses make him seem middle-aged and nerdy in a way she had never really noticed before. He is actually somebody's father, somebody's husband; and yet he is sitting here with her at the Plaza, acting like a bigshot. He is rattling on about some boring case he is concerned with back in beautiful Pittsburgh, the most scenic city in these United States, built at the intersection of three mighty rivers. Emily feels a miserable nauseous revulsion settling in. How could she ever have gotten involved with such a man, an aging jock, a swaggering locker-room whizkid with his charming split-level and his tennis vacations and his $200,000-a-year income. God, she is a sucker. Any high-school girl could see he is a liar and a fraud.

"Did you know that after the war—World War II, I mean—they kept testing atomic bombs in the desert? They tested them all the way through the mid-fifties without taking any precautions about radiation exposure to resident populations in the West."

"Really!" he says. "I didn't know that. That's amazing."

"A lot of innocent people might have been exposed to radiation without even knowing it."

"Why did they do it?"

"Maybe they didn't realize how dangerous radiation was in those days—I don't know. They had a great new weapon—what did they care about a few thousand innocent people?"

"They *should* have cared—they could be in for the biggest lawsuit in U.S. history."

"You *would* think of that."

"Well—who wouldn't? Law can be an answer to injustice, after all. It's not just about lawyers making money."

"But even if those poor people could win, if they're going to die anyway, it doesn't really help them very much, does it?"

"Life is short. They should get what they can *while* they can—otherwise there can't be any justice for them."

"I wouldn't call that justice, I'm afraid."

"Sometimes justice is relative," Tom says.

"Did you really say that?" Emily says.

"Yep."

"Is that what they teach you in Law School?"

"It's what the world teaches you *after* Law School."

"I'm not sure I approve of you."

"Well, I approve of you, Emily—every square inch of you."

"When your wife called last night and I left the room," Emily says, "you didn't even call me to say goodnight. 'What am I doing here?' I asked myself. 'This is not *me*. I don't want to be this person. I don't like myself as this person.'"

"I'm sorry—I would have called. I thought you wanted to go to sleep." His smugness is terrifically irritating. He is nothing but a slimy lawyer making his case, a heartless philanderer and liar.

"I think we should end it," Emily says, surprising herself.

"Are you joking?" He puts down his fork and stares at her in disbelief through his nerdy glasses.

"I'm not the kind of person who *does* things like this."

"We're in love, Emily. What's wrong with that?" He looks injured.

"Hah!" That got his attention all right. The waiter approaches with his flask of hot coffee. Since they offer no resistance he pours both their cups full, while they sit stiffly and watch the bubbling and the fog of aromatic vapor rising out of each pouring.

"Well?"

"We're already married to other people! It's a sin," Emily says, emphatically.

"A sin? Come on." His mouth twists with frustration.

"Well, isn't it?"

"Sorry, I don't believe in sin, Emily."

"Well, I don't either. But if I did, this would certainly qualify, wouldn't it? It's so damned dangerous. It's so irresponsible. How could we be doing it?"

"I don't know—we're doing it. I just think we're trying to get through our lives with the minimum of agony. We're trying to find a few moments of happiness."

"All right, fine! If we are, I think we chose exactly the wrong way to go about it."

"I'm sorry you feel that way."

"I'm sorry, too. I wish I could be better at this. I really do. I wish I could enjoy it more. I'm just not cut out to be someone's mistress."

"You shouldn't think of it that way," he says.

"Why not? We might as well tell the truth. That's what it is!"

"But we have such a good time together, Emily. I have more fun with you than with anyone I know."

She wishes she had the energy to punch him. Maybe he would wipe that sleazy smile off his face. "That's your trouble, Tom, my friend—all you want from me is a good time. And I sure do deliver, don't I?"

"I don't follow you."

"You're just so goddamned casual about it, it kills me."

"Emily, I didn't mean it *that* way."

"How the hell did you mean it? Your true feelings just accidentally slipped out, is that it?"

"Oh, for God's sake," he says.

She really should sock him one. "This is just exactly the way I knew it would end up with us."

"How's that?" Tom says.

"As a casual relationship. You don't really care about me!"

"Of course I do. Why do you think I came all the way to New York to see you if I don't care about you?"

"Oh, you care about me to that extent. I'm good for a couple of nights at the Plaza. I'm a ball for that. I'm more fun than anyone I know."

"Oh, Emily . . ."

She gets up from the table and throws the crumpled-up napkin at her plate and stalks out while Tom waves his hand frantically, trying to attract the waiter. She hurries upstairs through the lobby, dodges past an astonished bellboy and into the elevator so that she can beat Tom back to their floor and lock herself in. (She knew there was a good reason she had insisted on her own room.) All she wants to do now is take a hot bath, lie down to rest for half an hour, then pack her bags. Then she wants to go home.

The phone keeps ringing while she is in the tub, but she lets it ring. Why is it that he fails to call when he should and then turns around and calls repeatedly when she wants to be left alone? She is so tired she could almost fall asleep here in the warm suds.

She gets up slowly, her head spinning dangerously, and decides to take two Excedrin—no, three. She swallows them quickly, then decides to take one more. She dries herself off and lies down on the bed across the damp towel, too exhausted to put on her clothes. The message light is blinking and the phone is ringing and her head is pounding. She never should have come.

She gets up and hastily packs her bag. Her head is starting to feel better and her heart is pounding. She enjoys walking back and forth in front of the mirror and imagines Tom watching her but not able to touch her or communicate with her. She does look so beautiful, flushed and smooth from her bath, glowing and alive. Her breasts are heart-breakingly lovely—they really are. Such a woman could drive men to . . . *All this beauty that was once yours, Tom, my boy—now out of reach. She didn't even have breasts when she was seven years old. Why would something that was not even there show the effects of exposure thirty-five years later? On the other hand, what did it matter? They could have her breasts if they wanted them. She was never going to get a chance to use them anyway. They were purely decorative, as far as she was concerned.*

She leaves quickly, closing the door so softly not a single mouse could hear her. She rides the deserted elevator down and prances through the lobby like someone with a mission. Outside, the day is drab and gray and miserably rainy. The doorman holds an umbrella for her, and a cab pulls up with a squeak of its brakes and a hiss of its tires on the wet street. She climbs in and the cabbie lifts her bags into the trunk. The trunk lid closes with a clank. Her door is just about to close when a man in a trench coat—Tom—comes out the revolving glass door of the hotel and sees her in the cab and moves quickly toward her.

"Start the car!" she wants to scream to the cabbie, but Tom is already bending down and climbing in beside her. Before she can get a word out of her mouth, the cab begins to pull away.

"Emily," Tom says, "why are you doing this?" Up close, his eyes are so bloodshot—he must have put the contacts back in—he looks almost like himself again.

"I'm too sick to be here," she says. He places his hand carefully on her shoulder.

"So you're going home?" he says, as if he can hardly believe it.

"Yes."

"Are you still angry with me?"

She is so furious she cannot speak or even look at him. She takes several deep breaths, staring straight ahead, where raindrops are dancing crazily on the hood of the cab, then lowers her head and starts to cry. Her heart is pounding like a kettle drum.

Tom puts his arm around her. "Oh, Emily, I'm so sorry. Tell me what I can do."

"Don't do anything! Just get out of the cab."

"Is that what you want?"

"Yes," she says, trying to sound convincing through her blubbering.

"I don't think you mean it," he says, patting her, kissing her wet face.

"Yes I do."

"I'll just ride with you to the airport, okay. Just as far as the airport. Then we'll say goodbye." She can't answer. She thinks of the skycap at the airport—milk and honey—maybe he would be there again today, saying silly, cheerful, suggestive things to every woman whose bags he lugs. She would like to plant a kiss on his smooth, shiny cheek and startle the daylights out of him. What would Tom make of that?

Then she will climb aboard the airplane and lift off and watch the island maze of the City getting smaller and smaller in the distance. *A huge shockwave rises out of the earth, and a gigantic oval of heat and flame and extreme pressure engulfs it all. Goodbye, New York. I never want to see you again.* Tom squeezes her to him and kisses her ear, her neck. *The bones inside her hand were outlined, as if she were seeing them on an X-ray machine; and as she watched, they changed from green to purple to orangish-red. Then it was too bright to see anything at all—except white.*

"Get out now," she says, a little breathlessly.

"All right," Tom says. He tells the driver to pull over. The cab comes screeching to the curb. Tom twists the door handle and cracks the door. "Is this the way you want it to end?" he says, looking sharply into her eyes with such a pained expression on his face that she even begins to feel a small sliver of pity for him enter her heart.

"Yes," she says, with conviction.

"All right," he says. He swings the door open and climbs out. She sees a triangle of wet pavement, breathes in the smell of rain and chestnuts and soggy newspaper, then the door closes and Tom is walking away, turning his collar up against the downpour. A great, suffocating vacuum seems to have entered the cab, seems to have filled Emily's throat like a small explosion.

The driver starts to pull away. "Wait," Emily cries out, too loudly. "Wait a minute," she says. "Pull over again, will you." The cab coasts back toward the sidewalk, where Tom is plodding along encased in his trench coat, not looking one way or the other, rain beating on his shoulders. He looks so sad, walking along, that Emily starts sobbing all over again.

"Miss?" the driver says. "Miss . . . where do you want to go now? . . . We need to make a decision here."

Her section of the plane is full of baseball players, well-muscled young men on their way to Columbus, she guesses, from the insignia on their jackets. The two Valium (or the Excedrin) have made her ears start to ring, but she is so calm and philosophical, she doesn't mind. Already she feels airborne, even before the plane has left the ground, and slightly dizzy, on the edge of some dream or hallucination. One of them stows a tall red bat bag in the compartment for coats, bending down to push it carefully to the back, checking out her legs as he kneels beside her armrest. "I'm taking good care of these babies," he says and winks.

"What are they?" she says.

"Tools of the trade," he says, "just tools of the trade. Mind if I sit here?"

"No," she says, "not at all. Is it your seat?"

"It is now," he says, which makes her smile for some reason. He has a broad, smooth face and a large, shapely mustache that makes him seem comical even before he says something. His mood is so hearty it invades her space like raucous music she is not sure she wants to hear.

She has a vision of herself as a very old woman, sitting alone in a rocker in a dusty room, straining to see out a foggy window, each pane crisscrossed with rain like the one next to her shoulder. Why had she been so cruel and unfair to Tom, a person she no doubt loves more than anyone?—even with his limitations—more than anyone.

When the plane takes off, pushing them into the seat backs, the ballplayer grips her hand in his and gently squeezes it. She is too weak to resist, but she is thinking now only of Tom and their future together. Later, when they have reached altitude, cruising through the high clouds, the ballplayer buys her a drink and begins to tell her about the major leagues. There are only six hundred people on the face of the planet, he says, who can hit a major-league curve ball and, luckily, he is one of them.

"What's your secret?" she says.

"It's easy," he says. "You have to give up your body completely. You have to convince yourself that any amount of pain is a small price to pay for a clean line drive. You have to want it so bad, you're willing to die right there."

Saving the Boat People

The Lieus, a Cambodian family, emerged from the Ohio Air commuter, slowly, timidly, all wearing the same Army-surplus T-shirts and enormous yellow numbered badges on their shoulders and backs. They must have been sorted out and numbered like cattle in the refugee camps. Now they looked like figures from some absurd game of human bingo, which, in a sense, they were, numbered not for the slaughter but for the opportunity to begin new lives; and, pathetically, the four children were barefoot and the adults, Mr. and Mrs. Lieu and the elderly grandmother, wore only cheap thongs on their feet, though the temperature hovered in the mid-forties.

The small welcoming group—Mr. Kennedy, the Methodist minister, the three other concerned village women, and I, clucking and smiling and making every effort to communicate welcome and brotherhood—quickly engulfed them and ushered the Lieus into the satisfactory heat of the waiting van.

SAANG
The metallic craft brought them to the earth again and through the plastic curtain she glimpsed a barren, desolate landscape more terrifying than any dream and all the color of death. The humans also were the color of death, the most hideous beings she had ever seen, like large pale slugs walking upright, waving their swollen limbs and baring their teeth strangely, as if upset or in pain. Surrounded by the giant pale-people, who resembled the enemy who had killed them and killed them, they were miserably frightened; and the landscape also was a horrible disappointment. The white air hurt their skins it was so white. How such creatures could feed their bodies from the dry, hard land was a mystery to her. They

seemed peaceful, but whenever they approached them, they showed their teeth like sick dogs and spoke an ugly language at them and one to another. "If the great fat male seizes my arm," she told herself, "I must not cry out." The baby began to wail uncontrollably as soon as he set eyes on the crowd of deathly faces hovering above him.

LESLIE

She does her stretching on the porch, laying her heel on the snow-scalloped railing and reaching for her pointed toe, then the other leg. Then the quads—catching her foot from behind, pushing it up her back. Bouncing on her toes, leaving a filigree of Nike tread-marks pressed into the powdery floorboards like the fossilized track of some as-yet-undiscovered species.

Out into the quiet, snowy street, taking short, quick, easy steps, as unobtrusive as a fox, just any middle-aged woman out jogging, correctly dressed, easily identifiable as—a jogger. Nothing desperate, sexual, or escapist about this, not at all. What could be a more socially sanctioned activity—twenty million people out here on the roads and walkways of the nation running off the pounds, thinning out the blood; and she is a part of it, the great running craze. A still-living representative of all those people from previous generations who used to carry the load of heavy physical labor in the culture, all the really good fieldhands and cartwrights and farmers and lumberjacks, the ones who were in some way sustained by the daily sweat and toil and fatigue of it and had passed on their genes to her—they were causing it, their instincts, their inheritance, their needs, finding expression through her body.

Beyond the rows of houses, she cuts down the familiar rutted country road, blue with snow and etched with the narrow runnels of cross-country ski-blades. In the fall, this trail was thick with ragweed and gold-enrod and Queen Anne's lace, the air spicey with the scents of pollen and new-mown hay. Now it is overlaid with white, the brownish stalks poking out above the crust, the only visible remnants of the dense vegetable spawning; and the air pinches the nostrils and nearly takes her breath away.

Her accident was . . . two years ago this fall, and she would never be the same. Tears spread back across her temples like the feathers on a bird's wing. No snow then—cars splashing trails of mist, slick asphalt, bubbles of drops clinging to the thick roadside grass like a coating of jewels, the rusty pick-up perpetually zooming down upon her like an avenging beast, the two unknown distorted faces gaping in the windshield. They had actually driven off the road to hit her. It had happened so suddenly she couldn't remember or hadn't seen what their faces might have revealed of their motives—contempt for joggers, hatred of women, random homicidal idiocy, drunken frenzy, or merely a slip of the wheel— she guessed she would never know, though she could never stop thinking about it. No motive—no motive at all—seemed plausible to her.

The blow spun her against the cab, where she struck the crown of her head, and then flipped her into the mushy loam of a cornfield where, when she awoke, she was staring up from the base of several gigantic stalks and the tassles overhead seemed to race across the sky like the traffic above an airport. Her rescuers carried her for miles, it seemed, up a cliff of pastureland toward the glowing lights of a dairy barn. She could neither walk nor speak and, by then, the pick-up was long gone. She thinks she remembers all of this exactly, but it may have been a dream— she lay in critical condition in a coma for four weeks and three operations, including brain surgery. She was to become a statistic, an official victim, and the subject of a stern editorial in the local paper about the need for additional caution among both joggers and motorists if such tragic accidents were not to become commonplace. She recovered, more or less, but the process was slow and painful, and the accident left her with a minor speech defect, not an easy thing to accept for someone with her previous verbal skills and energies. It is this incident, and its aftermath, her husband Jerry says, that give Leslie such a "unique capacity to empathize with suffering humanity, with victims of every sort."

Another mile or so and she will have exhaled as much of Jerry's Benson & Hedges pollution as she is likely to get rid of in one day's struggling, the superficial layers only, and already she is imagining with powerful vividness the desperate little alveoli in her lung tissue, each like a small choking mouth gasping for air and slowly, inexorably, filling up with a pool of tar like a dark tear.

SAANG

The larger woman has eaten the food of many people, yet she seems not to be troubled by this. Her arms are as thick as four arms, perhaps five arms. And there are others like her, many others. Even the thin people, like Less-lee, are so robust, so well fleshed. Where would they find the harvests, the abundance for such heavy eating in this barren land? Where do they find the food to fatten even their dogs? Each family in the village keeps a fattened dog as if to boast of their excesses. My very dog is fatter than your very dog. What can this mean?

Yesterday, we were taken to a building called the Supper-Market, where they had piled food to the ceilings in every row. So many little colored boxes, and bright lights shining from every corner of the room.

Huge tables covered with slabs of red meat many layers together, enough to feed us all for months! As quickly as the people remove the goods from the shelf or table, men in white gowns rush forward from behind the butcher-door to replenish those very items. At first I thought they must have a very huge warehouse in back of the butcher-door, but if so, it is nowhere visible from the exterior. I often worry about what may be behind the butcher-door at the Supper-Market.

We have brought home so many sacks of food, it required two of the wire carts to transport them to the Ford. We have taken perhaps too much for our share and the people might realize now that we eat too much and send us back to the Thai-camps. I cannot comprehend why they would want to give us so much food at once right at the beginning before they have seen us work. I sometimes have a very deep fear that they are fattening us all up for some purpose I do not wish to think of.

Leslie

In the early stages of her negotiations with the church, Leslie received an anonymous phone call during which she was told that if she insisted on pursuing her idea about bringing refugees to the village, one day she might come home and find a pile of charred rubble where her house used to be. "First it was the Blacks in this country, wanting a free ride, now the Cubans and Mexicans and Chinks. Every refugee you bring in, it takes a job away from a legalized citizen. Don't you do-gooders understand that?" He hung up before she had a chance to reply—just some miserable and ignorant hungover man who wanted to express an opinion. She wasn't ready to take his threat seriously, but it did make her more sensitive about public opinion and her obligation to persuade people of the rightness of what she was doing. One day in the grocery store she overheard someone in the next aisle saying, "Why can't we just send the money to the refugees and let them stay in their own country? For God's sake, why do we have to bring them over here? This is too far north for them. They'll never fit in here." Leslie hurried around the row of shelving and confronted the two women: "Look," she said, "they've la-la-lost they're country. Th-th-th-there's no place but here for them to go." On her way home, she passed a pick-up with a gun rack across the back window and a bumper sticker that read: HUNGRY? EAT YOUR FOREIGN CAR. It was a bad day.

She knows that the unspeakable, the unarguable, the crushing fact is—Jerry no longer finds her sexually attractive. Since the accident. He no longer sleeps with her. Lately he has begun discussing the social and philosophical merits of open marriage. The sense of alienation is almost palpable and getting worse, and she doesn't know why this has happened. She is the same person, isn't she? He seems upset by her running, by her refugee project, by everything that gives meaning to her life. He disguises his contempt for her under a cloud of solicitous concern. "Hadn't you better just take it easy for a while longer?" "Let someone else save the boat people. Why does it have to be us? We have our own problems." Or, after two cocktails, "If you hadn't gone to that silly liberal school, maybe you wouldn't have turned into such an insufferable bleeding heart."

In fact, he is such a prude, he is undoubtedly embarrassed by her running and, also, by the public exposure of her rescue project. He doesn't like the idea of *his* wife appearing all around town in nothing but her sheer nylon running briefs or her wet-look Gortex and sweatband like a savage, ecstatically pumping endorphins. Or maybe he doesn't want her to reveal her sweating thighs or cheeks, in case his golf or drinking buddies might be watering their lawns or shoveling their driveways at a particular hour. But, surely, if he knows *anything* about her, if he has learned one single truth about her character after fifteen years of marriage, he should know that she *must* continue to run after what has happened to her, she *must* do it, and she must carry her rescue project through to completion. It is not merely the result of "misdirected maternal instinct," as he has claimed, that she feels compelled to contribute to the relief effort. How absurd! The greatest amateur psychologist of our time always has a conveniently pathological explanation these days for all her motives and hopes.

LESLIE'S JOURNAL, DEC. 1ST

Impressions during first few days: The house seemed to please the Lieus, though they are obviously still confused and distracted from their long ordeal. The small, white clapboard house is on a quiet street, Elm Street in the village, and the rental is being supported by donations from the community and the churches, though the churches have been somewhat less helpful than I might have imagined. We have enough to keep the house for only four months—a fact I am keeping to myself—and I am counting heavily on the further generosity of concerned members of the area and the appeal of the Lieus' presence itself to generate other contributions to their overall support. In an emergency, the small side-porch might be rented out as a separate apartment to help defray expenses, though at present it seems best not to complicate the Lieus' adjustment by inviting strangers to live so nearby. These people deserve privacy and quiet and space after the anguish they have endured. Eventually, we must find work for Mr. Lieu. We must find other, better ways to stimulate people's altruistic impulses. This is our personal contribution to the betterment of humanity, to take on an individual, manageable portion of the world's affliction. We must see that these helpless, frightened little people can survive and prosper.

Further impressions: Though the language barrier is such a problem for all of us, we are slowly growing to understand the Lieus. When we returned from the grocery today, for instance, I was especially touched by Mr. Lieu's behavior. The man refused to eat until after all the children had been fed. (I wonder how often he has gone hungry?) We, of course, tried to convince him that there was enough food for everyone. But then we began to see that it was a matter of principle with him. Eventually, he did eat a small portion of Minute Rice.

Later, I was equally surprised by little Koki. When Judy Wheeler and I began to comb the little girl's hair, the hair kept coming out in alarming tufts in the comb. Finally, we smoothed it out and clipped it with a small barrette and held Koki up to show her how she looked in the bathroom mirror. I've never seen such a look of astonishment on anyone's face. It was almost as if she had never seen herself in a mirror before that moment. At other times, she has a deep, pensive look, a look too old, too experienced, for her small face. I suppose the most horrible sight that most of the local children have ever seen is, say, a nightcrawler squashed on the sidewalk or something unreal from a horror film. But these Cambodians, those little dark eyes, oh, my!—what *they* have seen! I hate to *think* what they have seen.

LESLIE

During her run, Leslie determines to try to improve things with Jerry. She will go by the office, she decides, and make a point of asking what he would like for dinner. She will be wifely and caring and see how he responds. Around five, she jogs to campus and into his building at the top of the quad. The halls are deserted at this hour. The students have wandered off to the dining halls, and the professors have all gone home, except for *her* husband. The fact that he is still here strikes her as additional evidence of his alienation from her rather than as proof of any special resolution on his part or dedication to his work. He doesn't *want* to come home. He would rather be here in this empty building, smoking and grading composition themes or taking a leisurely gander at *The New York Times,* as if *The New York Times* could tell him anything essential about his life or about their lives together. A wave of self-pity bends her mouth as she moves lightly up the steps to the second floor, trying to nurture a sense of buoyancy she does not really feel.

The door to his office is slightly open, and she sees immediately that he is, in fact, not alone. Someone wearing a shapely pair of ankle-strap pumps is sitting across from him, swinging her foot ever so slightly below her crossed legs. Leslie stops abruptly, out of sight, focusing on the arrogance and presumed familiarity of the gesture, puzzled at first, then alarmed that she might be seen, either by Jerry and the girl in the office with him, or by somebody coming unexpectedly down the hall, where she would be seen standing, appearing to eavesdrop. "I'm not taking anything for granted," the girl is saying.

"I'm not either," Jerry says. "I know I *like* having you around, Debbie. If you think I'm going to be turned off by your silly cock-teasing games, you're wrong."

"That wasn't the idea," the girl is saying, "not at all."

Leslie sways quickly back the way she came in and flees softly and quietly down the stairs and out of the building into the chilly anonymous darkness of snow-plowed walks, where she pretends to be jogging again with some definite destination in mind, bouncing up and down foolishly like some frisky adolescent, as her pounding heart takes a nose dive. If she runs far enough now, her mind will be a large empty window, a vastness of rolling white like the moonlit fields outside of town at midnight, and she will not have to feel or think anything about what she has just seen and heard. She will not have to feel or think anything at all.

SAANG

We grew and harvested acres of rice, but the crop was collected by Pol Pot's soldiers and hauled away. The Khmer Rouge told the people in Siem Reap they were sending the rice to Battambang. But in Battambang they collected the rice and told the people there they were sending it to Siem Reap. We never knew why all the rice had disappeared. Some days we had to divide one cup of rice fragments among a hundred people. We ate grass and roots and mice and insects. We saw which flowers the horses ate—and we ate flowers. We ate like animals. Some turned *into* animals. I know mothers who ate their dead babies. Almost everyone ate human flesh.

There was a madman in the village who always had a secret supply of meat. My mother used to trade tobacco and gold with him for a few pieces of fat to add to our soup. One day Pol Pot's soldiers broke into this man's house. There were more than sixty human corpses inside—some partially carved up and still bloody and covered with flies—and piles of bones stacked about the rooms and an enormous wealth of gold and trade goods. While the children of our village looked on, the Khmer Rouge beat the man until his skull was a pulp on the floor. Then they looted the dwelling and burned every trace of it with flame-throwing rifles.

If we had not escaped this madness, we would surely have perished or gone insane. In the darkness of night in the United States, I often remember the small boat that transported us across the Mekong to Nong Khai—its very drift and creak. We had walked for five days and nights. We feared the fisherman would awake and discover us as we pushed his boat into the dark waters. My sister, Vathana, had been shot to death in such a place, her body poured out on the bank of the river, where the family later came to cremate her, chanting somber prayers and weeping. Therefore, Vathana was much in my mind as we floated across the Mekong that night. The body of my small brother Koy, who also tried to leave with Vathana, has never yet been found. I imagined that the face of young Koy was there too beside Vathana's under the current. Other dead bodies were already swimming there and brushed against our low bow, soft and horrible as squid, or perhaps some were only branches or debris in the black waters, though they seemed to be begging to crawl in with us. When the baby began to cry, I stuffed his mouth full of rags to muffle the sound. I hardly recall the landing or how we later came to the camp, only the groaning of the boards of that small, clumsy boat, the mist, and the frightening quiet and the stillness of the souls upon the water.

Later, I learned that—as punishment for our escape—my relatives were killed by the Khmer Rouge, more than forty people—my father and mother, all my remaining sisters and brothers, uncles and cousins. All were murdered or starved to death. I and my children are the only members of my family left in the world.

In the morning light, we left the boat in the tall grass, collected our few belongings, and walked off down the long road. We had eaten nothing in three days, and could barely walk, and were without rice, fish, silk, or gold for trade. As we came near to the Thai camp, we heard shouts in the distance and, slowly ahead, as in a mirage, hordes of men, dressed all in blue jeans and blue jean jackets and wearing cowboy hats, were yelling excitedly and holding up chickens for sale by their scaly feet, and plastic blow-dryers and French perfume bottles and boxes of Thai cigarettes at $20 each pack.

LESLIE

Leslie is running quickly along the village streets on this cold, clear night after nine, a slender figure in a dark blue running suit with silver reflective stripes. The points of the heels of her running shoes are also reflective, so that whenever a vehicle approaches within a certain distance of her, its headlights arc back from her moving body and the driver sees a luminescent figure advancing or fading away, its limbs glowing or sparkling eerily, like some heavenly or extraterrestrial visitation.

LESLIE'S JOURNAL

The children have been sick for several days now, especially little Koki, and I have spent the last two nights looking after them, sleeping on the side-porch and getting up in the wee hours to sponge their foreheads, take temperatures, spoon out medicine, and comfort them. The symptoms are cramps, abdominal upsets, fevers, and sweats. Saang has these same symptoms, too—sometimes even more severe, in fact; but, according to Dr. Goldberg, it is nothing but an array of intestinal parasites they most likely picked up in the Thai camps, where the sanitary conditions are so notoriously poor.

Unfortunately, their condition did cause a problem at school. Some of the local children started making fun of Koki and the others when they would double up in agony and run for the restroom. Young children can sometimes be brutally cruel. Several of the teachers were concerned that whatever the Lieu children have might be contagious. Hepatitis and typhoid fever have been mentioned in rumors and have led to a certain amount of pointless hysteria.

Update: Saang and the children have responded well to treatment and are feeling much better now. This will be my last night on the side-porch, and I am almost sorry to leave. Why is it that helping these people seems so important and so gratifying to me? Taking the medicine in to Saang last night, as she rose up out of the covers and waited for me to pour the syrup into the spoon, I noticed for the first time really how exceptional her face is, how truly beautiful she might be when her health returns. It is a benign, exotic beauty, like that of some forlorn and forgotten, almond-eyed Asian princess, and almost frightening when one considers how far she has come to this place and under what circumstances and, by contrast, how alien and ugly we must seem to her. What can she possibly think of us?

LESLIE'S JOURNAL (CONT.)

We have been fortunate to secure work for Mr. Lieu—Kyheng—as a dishwasher at the Evergreen Inn. The salary is not much, but it should certainly help; and, more importantly, it should help give the Lieus a greater sense of self-sufficiency and involvement in the life of the community. Also, it will inevitably cause the people of the town to appreciate the sort of industrious, deserving family they have brought into their midst. The Lieus want to make their own way. They have a resilience and determination that is remarkable to behold. I'm sure they will be an asset to the town, and their story might make it easier to resettle other refugees in locations such as ours.

Language is the hardest ongoing problem. Judy Wheeler tutors Mr. Lieu three times a week, but his progress has not been as swift as that of Saang and the children. He is by temperament a very shy, private man. Because of that fact and the nature of his work, he will have little opportunity to practice what he has learned. If he is ever going to find better work, however, which I am sure he is capable of eventually, he will need to know more English.

LESLIE

Leslie often spends evenings with the Lieu family. Kyheng, who has spent the day washing dishes at the Evergreen Inn, is now finishing up the dinner dishes. He reminds her of a porpoise—his hands splashing in the water and the dark gleam of his hair. At the same time, the stiff formality of his face and neck is very unlike a porpoise. Once, when she was trying to explain a joke to him, he suddenly understood—either what she was saying or the essence of it—and his face was transformed by crow's feet into a look of boyish hilarity.

Someone from the Church has donated a small black-and-white television set for the Lieus, saying, "This will help them learn the language and give them quicker insights into American culture." Leslie is not so sure these are insights they wouldn't be better off without, but she has delivered the set and helped show them how to turn it on and adjust it. The Lieus seem quite amazed and grateful. Apparently, they had never seen a TV set up close before.

Leslie sits quietly in the darkened living room admiring the little family as they watch their TV set. She has made this possible. They are such innocent, deserving people, and such a close-knit family. Saang and Kyheng are particularly close. Occasionally, Leslie has seen the two of them in town, on the street together, has seen the way they have of sharing a look without uttering a word. But, after all, they are strangers in a strange land and have no other face, no other responsible person (except her) to turn to and share a feeling. She can sometimes feel the spirit that must be between them. She envies it. She does not envy them their fates—of course not that—but she does envy them for their closeness and selflessness.

When she leaves, they are watching a rerun of *Jaws*. She hopes it will not give them nightmares. They are so hypnotically involved that they hardly notice she is walking out the door.

SAANG

The large fish with many teeth tries to eat the people. The picture of the fish was taken while it was swimming in the Atlantic Ocean. The picture was piped into a tower and propelled out into the air over many miles. The picture slides through the clouds alongside the several airplanes until it arrives into the plastic window of our TV network box. All of the people who swam in the Atlantic Ocean were eaten or killed by the huge fish, which is larger than a boat.

LESLIE

After two miles her legs feel ripe with blood, flushed and taut, and her movement as lubricated and smooth as a well-oiled engine. But she is not an engine. She is flesh and blood, warm, palpable, living. A living thing. A living creature, running now along a country road with a primitive sense of freedom as the wind blows against her face. A person, like any other, somewhat better educated and focused than most perhaps, somewhat more determined to impose her will upon the world—the inert, blind, stubborn, pitiful world. But *no more deserving* for the luck of possessing brains and an expensive background—not at all. *More responsible.* A duty to serve the good of the species as a whole. "Be ashamed to die until you have won some victory for humanity." She knows the human significance of these words. She understands them at some organic or cellular level. Her life is posed in a precarious balance, waiting to fulfill this particular mission or calling—to perform some act of charity or devotion large enough to qualify as a victory for humanity.

SAANG

The sick woman has a pill in her hand, and after eating it she feels much better. Many very happy people drink Coke, and beer delivered by horses with huge feet. Several men like to shave their faces with buffalo curd. Then they run back and forth bouncing a ball and shouting at one another.

LESLIE

The waitress takes Leslie's order to the kitchen, where Kyheng is visible behind the counter. He does not notice her in the dining room. He seems to be racing someone to see who can finish the dishes first. Occasionally, he growls sideways, or seems to, though no one is there. Then his eyes return to his hands, flushed in the scalding water. The boss likes him, the waitress tells Leslie, because, besides being a hard worker, he never complains and never flinches or talks back when being yelled at. The waitress does not know of Leslie's connection to Mr. Lieu. She thinks

Leslie is just curious. "Sometimes around happy hour, some of the men get after him," the waitress says. "They call him Small Pot. They don't like it that he has a job and some of them don't. But Lou"—Lou, she calls him—"doesn't pay any attention. He just smiles away and keeps on washing dishes. I think he understands a lot more than people give him credit for," the waitress says. "I think it's a wonderful thing that he came to this country," she says, "to be free like the rest of us."

After she finishes her lunch, Leslie goes to the kitchen to say hello to Kyheng. She is relieved when he gives her a toothy grin and seems honored to see her. She lays her arm in a maternal way around his shoulders and starts to say something fatuous about the dishes when suddenly she finds she is crying heavily into the moist neck of his shirt and he is clutching a dripping cup against her sweater, blinking in surprise, and trying hastily to back away and detach himself.

SAANG

I use a tub and washboard from the church-people to clean our clothes. The water flows from the spigot already hot, and the suds from the box are thick and full of foam. The strange fragrance from the powerful soap hurts the nostrils. My fingers become red in the scalding soapiness. I rush to hang the clothes on the line before darkness enfolds. My hands grow stiff in the white air, pinning up the wash I can barely see. In the morning, when I go out in the yard to collect these very same clothes, I scream. The shirts and dresses and pants have turned to plastic in the night, or perhaps it is white wood. They are glued to the rope, and when I pull them away, the plastic breaks and falls in small knives across my wrists. I run inside sobbing to tell Kyheng that our clothes have been forever ruined.

When Less-lee knocks, I tell her dreadfully of the mishap of the clothesline. She understands and is never angry. It will be all right, Less-lee says. We must take the clothes to a place called the Laundry-mat, she says, in the wintertime. She goes outside to look, and we put the hard clothes into a basket and into the backseat of her Ford.

The Laundry-mat is a large room with rows of white plastic machines and round windows in the walls, like the ones of the airplane, looking out onto a dark hole, and the burning smell of soap, ticklish in my nose. Together, Less-lee and I unsnap the airport window and fold the clothes into what seems a sideways tub. Less-lee puts coins into it, and suddenly the clothes begin to turn and bounce and the machine makes a rumbling. Less-lee squeezes my shoulder and we stand together a long time and watch the hard clothes jump inside the airport door.

LESLIE

The doorbell rings and Jerry goes to answer it. He stands for several minutes jawing with someone in the doorway.

"Who is it?" Leslie says, assuming it is one of his students, maybe the girl from his office.

"Old Professor Henry can't find his cat. Have you seen it?"

"No."

"He thought you might have seen it out on the trails somewhere, jogging along."

"Very funny. No, ba-but tell him I'll keep an eye out for it."

He returns to the door and talks further with Mr. Henry. The old man is a retired English professor who lives across the street. He wears a trench coat and a beret and walks his overweight, beige-haired cat on a string and secretly encourages it to defecate in the yards of neighbors who are not at home. When the cat escapes, he hunts for it with desperate determination; but the cat always comes back eventually.

Later that day, Leslie jogs over to Elm Street to visit the Lieus. Her legs are strong and eager and the short run feels good. The sun is out, bright on the fresh snow, and the yards shine as if encrusted with tiny diamonds. The Lieus are bustling about in their kitchen, looking happier than she has seen them in some time. An odd smell fills the house, and Kyheng smilingly shows her some hideous thing, something not-quite-chickenlike roasting in the oven. "Where did you ge-get it?" Leslie says to Kyheng, uneasily. "Where did the meat ca-ca-come from?" Kyheng looks to Saang for help with an answer.

"He catch," Saang says. "Set trap for small animal." Saang points proudly to a curl of bloody beige hair resting in a newspaper on the countertop. The truth of the matter hits Leslie with a sickening sense of certainty.

"Oh, my God," she says.

"We save money," Saang says.

"Oh, no," Leslie says, "this is a mistake. You must not tra-trap animals in town. Ma-many people have small animals as pets. They will not ap-approve of it, and there are laws against tra-tra-trapping in town. This is something Kyheng must not do e-ever again."

"Not in our country," Saang says.

"But in this country it is so. It is believed very strongly in Ohio. I will have to explain what has ha-happened to the man who owns this cat. He will be very angry."

Saang addresses Kyheng, explaining about the cat. The expression on his face goes from openness to astonishment to abject regret and guilt. He babbles something incomprehensible to Leslie and rushes to the oven, throws open the door, and pulls out the pan with the cat-carcass, burning his hands, and slamming it into the counter. The cat rolls out of the pan just as Kyheng releases the hot metal handles and drops everything with a crash in the middle of the kitchen linoleum and then quickly turns and runs cold water over his hands from the nearby spigot. He stands there, shaking his wet hands like fluttering birds over the sink, afraid to look at anything but the cat-carcass and pan in the middle of the floor. He is the picture of a contrite man, and Leslie can't help feeling sorry for him, though she turns away, suddenly queasy in her stomach. Saang, scolding Kyheng loudly in her native language, begins to pick up the mess, carefully using a folded dishrag as she bends to grasp the spongy carcass and place it in the pan and sop up the puddle of grease.

Surely it is her duty to tell Mr. Henry what has happened to his cat. "These people are from a simple agrarian culture," she will tell him. "They are good people. They did not understand what they were doing. They thought they were being thrifty, causing less of a hardship for their sponsors and the town. They acted as they have done before in order to live—by trapping game." But Mr. Henry will not understand. He will be terribly injured by what has happened. The memory of the ugly hulk of the cat's body in the oven keeps passing through her mind. Then she sees it fall sickeningly to the floor. The cat was the old man's only companion. How could he possibly forgive her or the Lieus or anyone for what has happened? It might be more merciful not to tell him. Then he will not have to imagine the horrible sight in the oven. Let him think the cat ran off and died of old age? Was she just being cowardly to think of it this way, just making it easier for herself, or would it, in fact, be more merciful? She imagines Mr. Henry coming again to her front door to inquire about his cat: She says, *I was just this very moment on my way across the street to tell you some very sad news.* Mr. Henry falls heavily to the porch floor and clutches at his heart.

She might tell Jerry about the cat—as a way of helping her decide what to do. He has sometimes joked about the old man walking his cat into their yard whenever they are away, as he does with the other neighbors, joked about the grass being killed by catpiss or coming home after a two-week absence to find the house surrounded by piles of cat feces. Jerry will probably find the situation amusing, or it will make him angry. "Now maybe you'll admit that you've made a horrible mistake in bringing them here," he might say. "Now maybe you'll admit for once that you could have been wrong."

SAANG

Many women have trouble with soap in their plastic machines at the Laundry-mat, and they squirt medicine into their noses and smile. Soldiers are lying in a ditch beside the road with bleeding arms and feet, and one man is missing from his head. Huge airplanes take off on the runway and fly at the sunset.

LESLIE

Leslie has a disturbing dream. She and Saang are out for a walk along the jogging trail. She sees a worried expression on Saang's face that bothers her, affects her mood, even under the surface of her consciousness where time is blown up like the microscopic view of a cell or shrunken as in a computerized aerial photo of the lunar landscape. She sees Saang walking into a web. She can tell that Saang does not know the web is there, whipping around her ankles. Leslie tries to explain it to her, but her voice is like a distant radio signal, fading in and out. Suddenly, the soil around them is dry and rocky and crawling with long-tailed rats. The rats have yellow eyes and ugly jaws and tongues like giant iguanas. Saang's feet drift an inch above their snapping, lecherous faces.

Leslie wakes up in a sweat. She reaches over to Jerry's side of the bed, but the bed is empty, the sheet cold. The digital clock says 1:58.

She gets up and pulls on her bathrobe and wanders down the hall to Jerry's study. No one there. She checks for a light on elsewhere, tiptoeing barefooted down the cold stairway, feeling her way along the bannister, then, arms outstretched, thin as a ghost in the darkness, reaching for the edges of the woodwork, the edges of the door frames. But there is nothing but blackness. A car rumbles distantly in the street, and reflected light passes across her face in the shape of a network of warped panes.

She falls asleep again: the asphalt steams in the early morning heat. The road goes on and on, past groves of maples, fields, crossroads, barns with cattle waiting sullenly for release. She passes a farmer's house and strides out into the open country. She is a long way out, perhaps eight miles, cruising steadily on her hot, slick legs. Up ahead, far up the long road, a dark brown pick-up turns lazily out of a farmyard and drifts toward her, the profile of its bulbous fenders squaring up with the sloping berm and fence rows. Then it accelerates furiously, the round lenses of its glassy headlights suddenly bearing down on her like the eyes of some gigantic mythical demon.

A dark cloud moves across the face of the sun, and the wind begins to stir the high grass. She is bounding down the center of the road, and the pavement is clear for miles ahead except for the brutal scarred grille of the pick-up, sweeping down upon her. She picks up her pace, sprinting now. She glowers at the faded hood, feels the rush of air, and sees, at the last moment, as the grille is actually striking her, that the driver is only her husband, Jerry, and Jerry's eyes look down at her and are full of regret.

When he comes in, she is still there in the darkness, doubled over, crying into the couch cushion, which smells faintly moist and acrid, like coats returned from the dry cleaners on a damp day; and then he is above her, leaning into her, patting her shoulder and crooning endearments into her ear that are nothing but lies, she knows, miserable lies, every one of them. How can he fail to realize that she could never, ever, be deceived by such self-serving, transparent lies?

LESLIE

She runs and runs, her feet drumming on the asphalt like pistons, like the metal thrusting parts of an oil rig, something mechanical and inexorable and indestructible. Something unremitting. Or another thing: anesthetized, falling, soaring, diving, like a wounded gull, like a lemming rushing to the sea and diving over the cliff wall. Soaring. The heat rises into her face and back, the flush and swelling of the blood, the sweat breaking out, the sense of timelessness and oneness with the earth. The pain and the absence of pain. She stops suddenly and walks, enters a grove of trees beside the road, far from any house or watching eyes. Some force has taken over her body now. It forces her to stop, to lean against this particular small tree, to press herself forward against its thin, hard living surface, while she tenses the muscles in her legs and buttocks and moves her fingers slowly over the tautness of the sapling and of her body. The oaky smell of the bark is a wildness inside and outside herself, an intoxication that carries her mind and breath away.

LESLIE

She can not live in the same house with him any longer, that much is clear. His presence is suffocating, nauseating. The energy required to deal with his presence, or the threat of his presence, with its stench of cigarette fumes and counterfeit pain, leaves her drained and pale and feeble. She has to find somewhere else to go. She realizes she has been thinking for some time that she might like to settle into the small sideporch next to the Lieus on a more permanent basis. She enjoyed the simplicity of the two rooms, the light from the high windows, the promise of comfortable solitude; and the idea of greater proximity to Saang and the Lieu family seems inviting, too. A chaste and sensible existence seems possible there, not to mention the additional appealing fact that the place is empty and available. She could be closer to the children to help mold them, to help teach them the language. . . . She could substitute at the school to contribute to the upkeep of the family. She gets out the Samsonite and begins packing energetically. The sunlight of a surprisingly balmy February day streams in across the bedspread, and she feels almost happy for the first time in weeks.

SAANG

Less-lee brought her suitcases and wishes to move onto the side-porch. She asks if this is okay with me. We sit in the bay window and discuss her upset. The lines near Less-lee's mouth are tight and sharp. Her earnest face is very thin. Less-lee's husband was not a good husband for a woman to have. Poor Less-lee is a miserable woman because of this plight. Less-lee cooks tea and we sit for a long time with the teacups and bread. Then Less-lee holds my face in her two hands and cries and places her head in my lap like a small child. We are trying to think of what to do next, sitting in the sunlight in the afternoon in our small house here in the United States of America.

Make Love Not War

When the GI returns to the World, he enrolls in a state teachers college in a small town in rural Ohio. He rents a three-room apartment above the hardware store on Main Street and hangs the Vietcong flag on a broomstick out his window. He smokes a lot of dope in his spare time, reads Vonnegut curled up on a studio couch alone in his rooms, and lets his hair grow down his back and around his face in smooth, soft, reddish-brown shocks. He washes and creme rinses his hair every other morning and combs it out in long, even flashes in front of the mirror, watching it bodying up around his fingers as it dries. His hair is so beautiful that he never knows whether the girls whose eyes are following him in or out of any classroom are admiring his build or envying his hair . . . or merely viewing him as a freak. He doesn't care. He wears twenty-five-dollar Western-style shirts with mother-of-pearl snaps and small, embroidered flowers around the collars and cuffs and delivers and picks up six shirts at the local laundry every Saturday morning.

The grunts like to fire at the tiny gooks who scavenge in the dump, pretending they are rats or insects. One day, on his way back to camp, the GI notices four small gooks huddled close together in a mountain of rusty cans eating something. As he draws closer, he can see what looks like blood on their mouths and hands and a fifth boy, the object of their interest, who has had the misfortune of having the top of his skull shot off. The injured boy (who is very much like the others in appearance) is still alive, his eyes open, but he is too weak to get up or resist. When the GI approaches, the four boys tense up and stare anxiously about—pieces of pink-colored brain-tissue still clinging to their lips and cupped in their hands—and then suddenly they leap up and run away. The cans scud and scatter. The GI can hear the grass move as the boys dart through it and away. Then silence. The GI slowly approaches the injured boy and peers curiously down at his ravaged head, marveling at how deeply the little rats have scooped inside, the enormous hollow they have left, delicate cords and tributaries hideously exposed. An involuntary thought crosses his mind like a revelation: *civilization really is necessary.* The GI removes his forty-five from his hip-holster and empties the clip into the small body, his ears echoing with each deafening crack.

The GI notices the girl immediately, the dark-eyed girl from his history section. She is the only girl in the bar with hair longer than his. "Dance?" he says. The strobe-lights ripple over her body as he follows her out to a clear place beyond the railing. When the music starts its deafening, concussive roar, she raises her arms above her head and begins to inscribe small circles with her wrists, as if she is writing his name backwards in the heavy air. Then she turns the other way, and they seem to swim together toward some unknown destination, as her hair swishes around her head. They are working in a field, threshing grain or hauling water, and the light of many days flickers over them.

The U.S. abandons the mountaintop LZ about two weeks before, storing ammunition there. So then the gooks sneak in, pull the pins on a cache of hand grenades, and depress and hide them under sandbags. You bump the sandbag and the spoon flies off and the grenade blows you in half at groin-level. The first two choppers that try to land are blasted right off the LZ. A couple of dumb grunts get creamed right away. The GI is one of the ones assigned to the disposing of the traps.

You probe underneath each bag with a bayonet. If you feel something clink, you jerk the sandbag hard away and kick the grenade over the side of the mountain and hit the deck. Sometimes it's only a rock and you bust the steel toe of your shoe and scare yourself shitless.

After they work the first day and clear most of the area, the weather goes bad. Rain and fog shroud the mountain in a viscous tissue of gloom. It is a week after his ETS, and the GI is still stuck on the mountaintop in the mud and rain. One morning the clouds suddenly evaporate and they are looking at an awesome blue sky. "All right," the lieutenant radios to base camp, "we've got a bright, clear zone up here. Let's get those Chinooks in."

"What Chinooks?" they say at base camp. "Who are you?"

"You fucking asshole!" the lieutenant yells.

Just as the Chinooks are overhead, the clouds close in again, as thick as gravy right down to the landing planks. The Huey pilot says he can't see a goddamned thing in the fog. They can hear the riffle of the chopper blades passing overhead, then disappearing.

"To hell with it," says the GI, "I'm walking home." He is halfway down the mountainside before they can catch up with him. . . .

The GI is really buzzed sitting in the classroom. He sees auras around the chairs and heads—a group of holy people sitting before the messiah. Only this messiah is no savior—he is a fraud—but the others don't know it yet. The GI stares out the window across a parking lot and half-a-lawn, waiting to hear the sound of choppers overhead, the whine and staccato of the blades, to airlift him out of there. *I'm going to get airlifted,* he thinks, and then chokes off a throatful of sour laughter with a poorly disguised coughing fit. He can almost see the underbelly of the Huey sinking toward him through the fog, and they are holding up little night flares to make a round target for the LZ. *Come on down, you mutha. Right over here. You gotta get me outa here, man.*

"Do you want to teach school?" the lieutenant says.

"Yeah, sure," the GI says.

They are stationed in the lowlands on the sea in a small fishing hamlet of delicate blue buildings, guarding a bridge to protect the village and the railway connection. The GI walks across the bridge and into town to ask permission of the hamlet chief. He is pulling night guard-duty, so with free time on his hands during the day, he might as well help teach the kids some English, why not? The chief seems pleased with the idea and introduces the GI to the schoolteacher, who is a young Vietnamese woman named Dang, recently widowed, who can speak English fairly well herself. They learn to play a kind of verbal baseball, shouting words back and forth across the classroom as the children listen and repeat, much of the time roaring with laughter—after which Dang translates. The children seem to greatly enjoy the game and the presence of the animated American, who knows all the funny words. Whenever the GI comes to the village, the children whisper, "Schoolteacher, schoolteacher," to their parents, and he is invited into their houses for soda and tea. "Come in here," they say and take him by the arm.

The GI begins to spend all his free hours with Dang, either at the school, strolling along the deserted beach, or at her small apartment. One day she offers him an elegant ceramic box. Inside are four marijuana cigars wrapped in banana leaves. She removes one and holds it out to him. He nods his head. Sitting cross-legged on her hammock, which is made from a Vietcong flag, she fires the joint with the American Zippo lighter she carries and they exchange puffs. She stares into his eyes and then suddenly unloosens the front of her dress and slips her shoulders free. "You like beaucoup?" *Yes,* the GI smiles—he likes her very much. He will never forget her.

Afterwards, she tells him what it had been like growing up in Saigon before she came to the village. Dang had been married to an ARVN pilot and they had had a six-year-old daughter who had been killed by a land mine. The GI tells her about the United States—about the Cincinnati Reds and high school and drive-in movies, and especially about rural Ohio, of which he is a native and which is a very beautiful place he wishes he might be able to show her some day.

When the GI returns to the village six months later, following an assignment in An Khe, nothing is left there at all but shattered empty buildings and blue rubble. The bridge is a skeleton of twisted iron. He finds the schoolhouse, empty and with its roof missing; and he finds the spot where Dang's apartment had been located, but it is nothing now but a large crater near a flat bulldozed area of shallow unmarked graves. Later he learns that while they were away some big brass had called in an American air strike, claiming the village was full of "VC sympathizers." For years afterwards, the GI has dreams about putting a forty-five to that colonel's head and watching it blow him away—over and over again.

The GI gets out of Vietnam on the fourteenth of June. Suddenly he is standing outside Oakland Air Force Base next to a wire fence at two in the morning staring at a beer-sign. *I am out of the Army,* he thinks. He takes a bus to the airport and flies to Chicago O'Hare and then to Dayton. Nobody knows he is coming home. There is nobody to meet him at the airport. He rents a Ford and drives home. It is one in the afternoon and nobody is home and the house is locked. He sits on the front doorstep and looks around. *This is wonderful,* he thinks—*I'm home.* He imagines how he must look, just sitting there quietly on the front stoop, out in the country, whistling, the bees droning in the shrubbery, the fields and woods rolling away toward the hazy horizon, the sun heating up the pantlegs of his dress-greens. *This is Ohio,* he thinks. *I'm here.*

• • •

The GI has trouble getting to sleep at night. When he first went to Nam, he imagined some ugly misshapen Cong gorilla silently creeping into his room at night or lobbing in a grenade. He barely slept for weeks. Then he became accustomed to the realization that there was really nothing he could do to prevent that from happening. He might as well stop dwelling on it and get some rest. If he woke up in the morning, fine. If he never woke up, at least he wouldn't have to worry about it anymore.

Now that he is home, the visions start to bother him again, which bothers him in itself. He felt he had dealt with all that pretty well. Now, all of a sudden, he wakes up in the middle of the night and finds himself down on his hands and knees in the middle of the throw rug yanking on the bedpost as if it is a mortar launcher. He keeps his forty-five loaded under his pillow. One night, when the girl raps softly at his door after midnight and lets herself quietly into the apartment, he nearly fills her lovely, shadowy body with forty-five slugs before he realizes his palm is wrapped around the revolver-handle like a piece of wet meat.

The next day he goes to a gun shop and buys three cans of Mace and lines them up on the bedside table like cans of spray deodorant and, with some misgivings, buries his service revolver in his footlocker between two blankets and his folded uniforms and his submachine-gun case and locks it up tight.

"Who owns this Dink flag?" someone yells from below. The GI gets up from the bed and moves to the front window and peers down, keeping his body protected behind the window frame. There are three of them, standing down in front of the hardware store in a certain way, feet spread apart in an attitude of bravado or ownership. Some local vigilantes, he guesses—probably vets themselves. He pushes the screen together and lifts it away and sits on the window ledge.

"Who wants to know?"

"You can't fly any flag but an American flag in this town," one of them says.

"Especially not that flag," another one says. "It's not legal."

"It's a free country, Jim. That's what I always thought anyway. Why don't you mind your own fuckin' business." The men cluster together in a tighter knot and talk among themselves. They all have short hair and seem too large for their clothes. One of them has a pack of cigarettes folded into the sleeve of his T-shirt.

"Take the flag down, asshole, or we'll come up there and do it for you," the one with the cigarettes says.

"I got a forty-five revolver up here that says you won't, chickenface."

"Who in the hell do you think you are?" he yells back.

The GI doesn't answer but climbs back inside and slides the sash closed. He unlocks his footlocker and takes out the buried forty-five and snaps in the clip, then returns with it slowly to the bed, where he flops onto his back, crosses his arms and sighs loudly—tucking the gun barrel snugly under his left arm—and commences to guard the door. It is clear to him that the flag has a different meaning to the locals than it does to him, but he does not feel he is obliged to explain that to them. To the GI, it is Dang's flag and an expression of his own identity. He went over there and brought it back. He seized it as a trophy from the enemy. He has earned the right to express his personal history in this silent, ambiguous way by possessing the flag and by flying it in his own window. When he sees it there, it reminds him of things he does not want ever to forget.

No one comes to the door. When he wakes up the next morning, the GI stares at the gun for some time, lying next to him on the rumpled bed-spread, before he realizes what it is or remembers how it came to be there.

The march on Washington begins with a long bus ride at night. They are mostly students and Vietnam vets and a couple of old people—Quakers—on the bus, and when they arrive on the outskirts of the capitol they begin to sing "We Shall Overcome" and "Ain't Gonna Study War No More" and other pacifist songs. But the GI doesn't join in and does not enjoy the singing. The girl wakes up and sings for a while but then falls asleep again in his lap. They disembark on a dark, tree-lined street, and all the people from their bus and other busses and cars are milling around the sidewalk in front of a church, people in denim and suede and army fatigues, bicyclists and back-packers, old people and cherub-faced kids. Inside the church, you are supposed to register, and they eat scrambled eggs and catsup on paper plates.

The march begins at dawn and attracts more and more people as it winds toward the White House and the staging area at Lafayette Park. There are vets everywhere with long hair and beards and medals: Silver Stars, Bronze Stars, Purple Hearts, and shoulder patches of the 101st Airborne, the 25th Infantry, the Big Red One, and others. Some are missing arms or legs. Some are pushing along in wheelchairs, or carrying squirt guns and cap pistols. At an intersection, a group of wildly singing and swaying people are seen holding butchered goats' heads and slabs of hearts high in the air and squeezing blood down across their faces and behaving like the walking dead. The GI digs his Vietcong flag out of his knapsack and ties it around his neck like a Superman cape. Thousands of them are moving down the street now with bamboo flutes, tambourines, balloons, and flowers, chanting and singing, waving flags and banners.

The view from Lafayette Park is of a White House surrounded by huge bright busses and cops everywhere wearing riot gear. The cops have white helmets and are strange and faceless behind thick plastic visors. One vet near the GI is collecting DD-214 forms as proof that the marchers are veterans. Someone offers him a glass eyeball. "Hey, Jack," someone yells, "how about a receipt from the Steam-and-Cream Massage Parlor in Bien Hoa?" A police wagon carrying a bullhorn slowly circles the park, instructing the marchers to disperse immediately. The familiar whir of helicopter blades intrudes overhead.

As they turn south toward the White House, riot police on motor scooters charge to break their line of march. "Hey, we've got a purr-mit!" someone says. Then, in unison, the chant begins, "Sieg heil, sieg heil, sieg hell." The GI starts to run with the others across the wide lawn but is tackled hard and rolled over and jerked upright by his hair. The flag slips loose from his neck and is trampled in the rush of stampeding feet.

He is a prisoner of war, trapped with thousands of others inside RFK Stadium, home of the Washington Redskins. The GI dreams the girl has come to rescue him. He leans into the retaining fence, hanging from the smooth wire like an imitation of Christ on the cross. Suddenly he recognizes the girl in the crowd milling about outside the detention area. She moves quickly toward him, her face intent, her hair lashing from side to side as she runs. She reaches her hands up toward the wire lattice to embrace him.

Times Square

The elevator doors open and a young woman, who is alone on the elevator, glances up at you and smiles warmly and says, "Hello," as if she knows you from somewhere. She is the first friendly person you have met today. You are in the lobby of the Times Square Hotel, so you expect her to get off the elevator. You wait politely for her to do so, before entering. But instead she hesitates, her hands resting on either side of her hips against the chrome railing at the back of the elevator. "Going up?" you say. She gives you a coy smile. You get on the elevator and punch your floor and back up against the wall. You are reasonably certain you have never seen her before in your life. There is a peculiar, unidentifiable tension in the elevator as you ride up together. She is apparently evaluating the cuffs of your pantlegs. You get off on the twelfth floor and return to your room to gaze out your dingy window at the airshaft.

You have made elaborate arrangements to meet a woman, an old girlfriend, here for the weekend. You have made a twelve-hour bus trip from Cincinnati to meet her and you are looking forward to seeing her tonight. She was supposed to fly in from Cleveland and meet you in the lobby of the Times Square Hotel at six P.M., but that was two hours ago. There is still no sign of her and no message for you at the desk, where you have checked several times and tried to elicit some modicum of concern. You decide to ride back down to the lobby and sit in one of the cracked leatherette lounge chairs in the cavernous space, which looks as if it belongs in an old Art Deco movie theater, and try to decide if you should give up and go catch a bite to eat. This time there is no one on the elevator but you.

She is either stranded in some airport, her plane crashed, or she decided against making the trip—she is in Cleveland watching TV with her husband or possibly washing the dinner dishes about now, her lovely hands moving through the warm water and suds. Or she is, in fact, here in the hotel. She has left you a message, but the incompetent hotel clerk misplaced it or threw it in the trash or put it in the wrong slot. You have asked about messages so many times that the clerk is getting irritable. Well, the clerk was irritable to start with. Now he is openly furious. He has an acute way of conveying the impression, without opening his mouth, that seeing your face bores him near the point of inducing homicidal frenzy. If you sit here a while longer, you think, she will come wobbling in through the front revolving door, and you will run right over and embrace her and say, "Where have you *been*? I was worried about you."

About nine you wander outside and stand for several minutes in front of the hotel, hoping she will pop out of one of the cabs passing by. Nothing of the sort occurs. You see a sign for the Dixie Cafe across the street, so you decide to eat something. You are feeling weak from hunger. You will sit in the front window and try to keep your eye on the hotel entrance. If she pulls up, you will jog over and say, "I'm having a bite at the local bistro."

The Dixie Cafe is not a bistro. It is a truly tacky coffee shop with a slab of blue counter in front of the grill and an array of blue tables and tubular chairs and light so white it damages the eye's watery membranes. You find a table and glance across the street at the hotel entrance, but the outside is dark and hard to see. The neon in the sign sizzles above your head. You didn't know the Times Square Hotel was going to be this seedy. You chose it from your old *Flashmaps of New York* book because it was within easy walking distance of the Port Authority bus terminal and you reasoned that any hotel near *The New York Times* couldn't be all bad. You obviously have a lot to learn about the City. You are exactly the sort of person whom real New Yorkers would make rude jokes about. You order the roast beef dinner with apple pie for dessert.

A young girl with a ponytail comes in and approaches the counter and starts talking to the cashier, an emaciated man about fifty with slicked-back yellowish-white hair. Everyone in the place can hear what she's saying. She says she just got in from Boston, Massachusetts, and she needs fifteen dollars right away to pay the rent. She's looking for work. She pauses to let this sink in and quickly scans the tables and the men at the counter while waiting for an answer. She has blue eyes, outlined heavily with black mascara, and shiny white boots.

"We don't have no work," the cashier says.

The girl says she will stay with him all night for fifteen dollars. The cashier says he can't but he knows a guy who will.

"Who's that?" she says.

"The cook," he says. The cook is not here right now, he tells her. He just stepped out for a breath of fresh air, but he'll be back in a few minutes.

"I'm in a hurry," she says.

"He won't be that long," the cashier says.

The waitress brings your steaming roast beef on a plastic plate. The meat is thin and tastes a lot like a frozen TV dinner, but you are so hungry, even cardboard would be delicious.

The girl with the ponytail is talking to some of the men at the counter, but you can't hear what she's saying. In a minute or two, she comes over to your table and sits down across from you.

"You want to spend the night?" she says. Her tiny dangling heart-shaped earrings tremble above the formica in front of you. "I really need the money and I don't feel like waiting any longer."

She makes an intricate gesture with her pink tongue that causes your eyelids to flutter strangely. You have a fresh mouthful of cardboard apple pie you are trying to finish chewing, but before you can say anything, this black dude at the counter turns halfway around. He has a goatee and is wearing a leather cap. He is holding a wallet in his hand and he shows her the corners of two twenty-dollar bills. The girl gets up and leaves with him. All this happens so fast, you are still chewing the same piece of pie after the door has swung shut behind them.

When you return to the hotel, a different clerk is on duty. But there is still no message in your box, whose location you have memorized. You don't even bother to ask. You perform a neat about-face and stroll briskly out the door again as if you know where you are going. Your body marches boldly toward the bright lights. As you turn onto Times Square and begin to move uptown, you suddenly remember a news item about a visiting history professor who refused to hand over his wallet to a mugger and was shot in the face. You suspect you may look like someone from out of town. You are afraid you could also be the sort of person who might part reluctantly with his wallet. You have been on Times Square several times, after all. Still, you wish you had not worn your best coat.

You duck into the Metropole Cafe and watch the dancing girls whirl above your beer. You wish you knew where Kathy was right now—the girl you were supposed to meet. When you dated in graduate school, she seemed to be a responsible person. She was a beautiful girl and you wish she were here. This is not exactly the way you had hoped to spend the evening.

You browse slowly through a pornographic bookstore on your way back to the hotel. Something strange is going on in back, where banks of garish lights are flashing and men keep filing up to a ticket window. You ask the man in the window what it is, and he slides change at you and says, "You need quarters." You pay for the quarters and go in through the curtained entrance, where you are confronted by a hundred black doors with little red bulbs above them. When someone opens a door and enters, the bulb goes on. You try it. Inside, you find yourself in a black closet with a coin machine. When you put a quarter in the slot, a shade opens in front of you, revealing a carpeted stage where several women are lounging, dancing, or moving seductively toward those windows where hands are waving dollar bills. You watch the nearest one. The woman takes the bill out of one of the hands and then allows the hand to softly, reverently touch the tips of her bare breasts. After a few seconds, she backs away and looks for another hand. Just then, your shade flies down.

You insert another quarter. The shade goes slowly up. Already the woman has moved slightly away from your window. You begin to notice that shades are going up and down continuously all the way around the elliptical stage. You suddenly understand what this is all about. You marvel at this innovative use of shade-winding technology. You try to make a rough estimate of the number of quarters-per-hour consumed by the many booths. Your shade flies down. You insert your quarter and wonder how many quarters this could take. The woman is really quite lovely. She seems to be enjoying herself, but how could she be? Your shade flies down. You insert another quarter and try to estimate how many dollars she might be making at this line of work. She moves toward your window. She seems to be looking at you. Your shade flies down. You begin to feel like Pavlov's dog. As you return to your hotel you are engulfed in a crowd of theater-goers—men in tuxes and stunning women with diamonds in their ears—getting into limousines.

The next morning there are two messages waiting for you at the front desk. The first one says: "Unexpected complications. Hope to see you soon. Love, K." The second one says: "Would you happen to know of a good place to eat?" The second one seems to be in the same handwriting as the first, possibly that of the desk clerk? You would ask, but he has disappeared into the back room after sliding the messages at you across the slippery desktop as if he were in a terrific hurry. No need to antagonize him further, since there might be other messages. As you walk across the lobby, you spot the young woman who rode with you on the elevator yesterday. She is making a beeline to intersect your path toward the street. "Oh, it's you," she says, stopping as if she has just now noticed you for the first time. Up close, she has strikingly beautiful, dark, wide-set eyes and an elegant nose with too much powder on it. She is wearing a long, shabby tweed coat and black flats.

"Are you heading out for breakfast now?" she says.

You say, "I thought I might."

"I've been searching for three days for a halfway-decent restaurant," she says, falling in beside you.

"I was just going across the street," you say. "It's just a greasy spoon. Probably not your style."

"When you're as hungry as I am," she says, "the closer, the better."

"I don't know about this place," you say. You amble across 43rd Street together, and you hold open the door of the Dixie Cafe. "See what I mean?" She smiles bewitchingly and passes in front of your arm as if you have just said something amazingly clever and are escorting her into the foyer of Trader Vic's. You notice that her lipstick is slightly crooked above her upper lip.

The tables are all full, but there are two empty stools at the counter. You sit down on one. She places her coat on the other and whispers that she has to go to the "little girls' room." Her perfume smells like a tropical night with tom-toms playing softly in the distance and a strand of her hair brushes your cheek. You blush and order some pancakes.

"I'm tellin' you, she was a doll," the cashier is saying. "She would have stayed with you *all night long* for fifteen dollars. How come you was late?"

"Sure," says a voice in the back. "Tell me another one, Harv."

"Would I lie to you? She comes in here looking for you, and she was a knock-out. You should have seen her. I think she must have heard about you from someplace." The cashier performs a wheezing imitation of laughter.

"Aw, Harv." A pasty-faced man wearing a large, puffy baker's hat appears from the galley, drops a plastic plate of pop-up-type pancakes in front of you, and struggles along behind the counter and pours himself a cup of coffee. He is a squat, bulbous fellow with enormous arms and a gorilla-like profile. Just then your friend returns and slides onto the next stool, touching your shoulder to steady herself.

"How come you was late?" the cashier continues.

"I wasn't," the cook says.

"That girl was a real tomato, wasn't she?" the cashier says in your direction. "He was here when she came in. He'll tell you. You was here, wasn't you? I thought I recognized you." You smile noncommittally. "He's no fool. He almost went with her himself. Ask him." He cracks up again.

"I have to find a drugstore," your friend says.

"Don't you want to eat something first?" you say. She looks at your plate of partially eaten pancakes and makes a face.

"Maybe I'll see you around," she says. She stands up and puts her coat on and pulls her hair out from the collar and carefully buttons each button and stares at the side of your head.

"I'm almost finished, anyway," you say.

She walks outside and hesitates for a minute or two in front of the plate-glass window and strolls back and forth as if she might be waiting for a bus. Once, when you turn around briefly to check on her, your fork still raised with its syrupy morsel near your mouth, you see she is staring at you close to the window, her hands cupped around her eyes to block out the light. Then she comes back inside and leans on the stool next to you, holding her thin lips to your ear. "You wouldn't happen to know where any drugstores are located around here, would you?" she whispers. "I haven't been able to locate a single drugstore around here for three days."

You walk her over to Seventh Avenue where you find a huge drugstore within the first two blocks. She doesn't seem to notice until you make a sweeping gesture at the door. She looks at you, at first, as if she always suspected you were a little odd and moves straight into extreme amazement and utter relief at what you have uncovered.

"I must have passed here sixty times," she says, kissing you dryly on the cheek. "I used to live around here."

"I've always been good at finding drugstores," you say.

"I'm not really sure I want to come back here, you know what I mean," she says. "I mean, I hated Miami, but it isn't easy to get back in the flow when you've been gone for two years."

"What sort of work are you looking for?" you say.

"You're cute," she says. "Have you got a picture of yourself? I'd like to have one for my wallet. . . ."

"Not with me," you say. "I'll have to send you one."

"Oh, I almost forgot," she says and hurries into the drugstore.

You kill some time in shampoos and creme rinses while she talks to the pharmacist. You have seen most of these bottles more times than you would care to think about in other drugstores. You have the labels practically memorized. Most of them contain formaldehyde, among other ingredients, to which you are philosophically opposed. You are no chemist, but you draw the line at pouring formaldehyde on your head. You wander down the aisle toward your friend, who is still engrossed in pharmacy. A large tube of something is lying on the counter in front of her. You try to get close enough to read what it is without seeming too nosey—some kind of "jelly," you think. She jumps when she sees you out of the corner of her eye and says urgently, "Put it in a bag! Put it in a bag!" She is two dollars short, so you pay the difference. You walk out together.

"Get everything you needed?" you say.

"Don't I wish," she says, making a little fist and pretending to hit you on the arm with it.

You walk aimlessly for a while.

"Maybe you could send me a snapshot, too," you say.

"I doubt it," she says.

"You wouldn't send me a snapshot?"

"I'm not sure I have any, is all," she says. "I have one that was taken of me about a year-and-a-half ago—in one of my costumes. In case you didn't know, I was a dancer. Actually, I have two pictures because I was supposed to send one to my brother and never did. I could send you that one."

"I live in Cincinnati."

"I've been working as a receptionist, but dancing is my true profession. The trouble is, how do you find a job? I can't exactly see myself on 'MTV,' can you?"

"I'll bet you can't guess what my profession is."

"Don't tell me you're an agent."

"I'm not."

"Thank God. . . . Are you a bookkeeper—what do you call it—an accountant?"

"No." You find this moderately insulting. You want to say, "Actually, I'm still in graduate school, working my way toward unemployment," but you don't think she will get the joke.

"I have to go back to the hotel now," she says. "I have an appointment."

"Do you want to have dinner or something?"

"We could talk about it later. You could leave me a note."

"I'm not having very good luck with notes lately," you say.

"Okay, then I'll leave *you* a note," she says. "But don't count on it. I never get very hungry at dinnertime." She turns and rushes off down the block, her coat flapping, her feet splayed out in an inimitable duck-footed gait in the down-at-the-heel flats. You wonder how long it will take her to locate the hotel.

On the way back, you stop to browse at a magazine store. You leaf through a thick guide to the *Restaurants of New York*. You buy the guide and a paper and wander among the shelves, pausing briefly in front of some men's magazines. You have long been of the opinion that a close analysis of the latest changes in feminine behavior exhibited in magazines might reveal major insights about American culture. You are unable to penetrate the mystery of exactly what today's message might be, except you realize suddenly that what you are seeing is a fantasy of permission. You wonder why it has taken you so long to figure this out. The most obvious quality of the women pictured is that they are all saying yes. Whatever their slight physical imperfections—which are few enough—you have always found this quality unspeakably charming. You realize with a slight shock that nine-tenths of the store is given over to parading this heartbreaking quality of willingness. "All right, gentlemen," the store clerk is chanting, "bring them to the register. This ain't the public library."

When you return to the Times Square, there is a Mailgram waiting for you. The clerk acts as if he is terribly impressed. You carry the envelope unopened back to your room, close and lock the door, and lie down on the bed to read it. You notice at the top that it was dictated and sent yesterday.

Mailgram c/o Times Square Hotel:

Dear Jimmy: I really didn't stand you up. I'm having a lot of problems right now. It probably seems that I'm always having problems—guess that's my whole life. I'll write more when I can cope. I'd never hurt you intentionally, you know I wouldn't. I had all intentions of being there, but Phil and I aren't seeing eye-to-eye at this particular time and the aggravation is really too much. Our marriage really isn't that strong, and it seems to weaken every day. I have asked him to leave, he won't, and so I go my way, and he goes his. It's a hell of a way to live, but I don't have the courage to leave and be independent, mostly because of the baby. I wish I knew what to do, but I don't. I'm sorry if I hurt you. It seems I do that quite a lot. I really never mean to.

Love Kathy

You don't feel that much like going out, so you spend the afternoon next to your airshaft studying your guide to the *Restaurants of New York*. You notice that the walls of your room are actually painted black, which, you decide, is not a cheerful color. About five you go down to the lobby, where you can see that no further messages have fallen into your mailslot. You spread out on one of the couches with your paper and lose yourself in the sports page. At some point you glance up and see your receptionist/dancer friend with the flats conferring with the desk clerk, except now she is wearing beige heels. She plops down next to you on the couch.

"I like your shoes," you say.

"Puerto Ricans who do something to their hair are still Negroes," she says, "whether they want to admit it or not."

"Are you sure that's true?" you say. She seems to be in a bad mood.

"Sometimes I wonder why I bother."

"We could have dinner together," you say. Her eyes pierce at you as if you have just offered her a hot watch. She is wearing a fresh coat of make-up and dark-red lipstick. She is not a bad-looking woman, you think, though something is peculiar about her chin. "My treat," you say.

"I can't stand the thought of eating meat," she says.

You are, after all, an expert on the restaurants of New York. You take her to a kosher, vegetarian restaurant.

When she takes off her coat at the restaurant, she is wearing a bright-red dress. She has no interest in the menu. The waiter enters and pours two glasses of water from a cutglass pitcher and cocks his ear for the order. He is one of those waiters who keeps it all in his head. Your friend sips water and says what she would really like is just a ham sandwich.

"Sure," the waiter says. "To go with your Gilbey's gin." He thinks she is joking.

"Don't you ever serve just plain ham sandwiches in this restaurant?" she says.

"This is a kosher restaurant, Lady. The only ham we have is shipped all the way from Israel. It's called Abra-ham." He laughs loudly.

"What about peanut butter," she says. "I'll just order a peanut-butter-and-jelly sandwich, I guess."

"The peanut butter is also from Israel," the waiter says and gives you a conspiratorial wink.

Back at the hotel, you ask her what her plans are for the evening. You wonder if she might like to go to a movie or maybe come up to your room and talk for a while. A young man with long hair and lugging a fluorescent backpack passes near her as you are talking and touches her on the sleeve. "Goodbye," he says. She seems surprised, turns part way around, appears to recognize him, and nods. He smiles, revealing several undersized, crooked teeth, and starts to leave toward the main revolving door, then returns and gives her a little hug and goes on out.

"Who was that?" you say.

"A friend," she says. "Just someone I met."

"I've been meaning to ask you," you say, "were you the one who put that note in my box yesterday?"

"Yesterday?" she says, and waves her hand to dismiss the question. "I have to go back to my room now . . . to change," she says.

"Okay," you say.

"Then I'll come down to your room after that."

You ride up on the elevator together. "Are you sure you want to?" you say. "You look tired."

"Aren't you going to your room now?" she says.

"I thought I'd take you back to yours first," you say.

She gets out her key and weighs this information. You step off the elevator together and walk down the long corridor on her floor. She walks you all the way to the end, then part of the way back. Finally, she stops in front of a door. "You'd better wait in the hall," she says, unlocking the door and opening it. The light is on. She goes in and leaves the door open behind her. You follow her in and drop heavily into the one chair. The room is similar to yours except for the make-up bottles on the dresser.

You say, "You want me to wait in the hall?"

She doesn't answer, just takes off her coat and then her dress and lies down on the bedspread. "I'm glad I ran into you," you say. She doesn't say anything. Her panties and garterbelt are embroidered with tiny rosebuds, and the seams of her stockings are crooked. She is very still, lying face down. You realize after a few minutes of silence and no reply that she has fallen asleep.

You sit for a while, just for the company. If she were awake, you would like to paste fifty-dollar bills all over her body—very slowly—if you had any fifty-dollar bills. If she insisted on a particular spot, you would be more than willing. She could point to the spot, any spot at all, and you wouldn't argue, you wouldn't complain.

The Weeds of North Carolina

He was a callow, idealistic, emotional young man who could not quite believe he had attained this pinnacle in his life. He was *in* college. He was a "college man." His idea of what college would be like, however, had been highly romanticized, as even he began to realize. He had imagined himself lodged in an opulent room with gold curtains and handsome leather-bound volumes arranged around the walls from floor to ceiling. He could see himself seated in his armchair, reading passionately, absorbing the wisdom of the ages without which no civilized man could consider himself well educated, pausing only occasionally to re-light his briar or tighten his rather good-looking jaw muscles as some particularly choice bit of lore registered in his consciousness.

As it turned out, his dormitory room bore little resemblance to this vision. It was a bare, cramped room with a diagonal slab of overhanging ceiling, painted an institutional green, and with one window, containing squares of wavy leaded glass, and one small bookshelf barely three feet high.

On his way around campus that first day on his own, he must have looked particularly lonely or disappointed or self-conscious. Two hulking upperclassmen in football jerseys glared at him with unexplainable contempt as he passed them outside the Union, and one of them tittered and said, "Oh, mama, I'm so homesick I can't *stand* it," in an insulting falsetto. He kept walking as if not realizing the remark was directed at him, but he was secretly furious. He was nearly as big as they were and had lettered in three sports in high school himself. How could they have known he was a freshman, he wondered. He certainly wasn't homesick, was he? He was sure he was not.

The one person from home he would miss was Julie Greenway, the girl he had been going with for over two years. He loved her—they had a cozy physical relationship—but he was relieved, in some sense, to be away from her for a while. They would write. They had made certain promises. She was going to Smith, an all-girls' school in Massachusetts with, Julie informed him in the letter that was waiting for him at the post office, the highest suicide rate in the nation (how did she *know*?), and the median income of the fathers in her intro-to-soc class was $75,000 a year (how did she know *that*?).

The freshmen inhabiting the room opposite his were not his idea of what to expect either. After walking around and slowly unpacking, he rapped on their door with the idea of introducing himself. The one answering his knock was an enormous, hairless, shirtless youth lugging a huge dumbbell in his free hand. He set it down hard on the oak floor with an elephant-like exhalation and offered what proved to be a knuckle-breaking handshake. "Kent Masterson," he said. "From Dallas. Pardon the sweat. I like to lift weights." He rested his arms against the doorjamb like one of the great apes. He was probably six-four.

"Moke Galenaille," Moke said. "From Cincinnati. I guess we'll be seeing quite a bit of each other. I live across the hall." Masterson made no effort to move back or invite him in.

"Nice to meecha, Galenaille. I'll be finished with my routine here in about fifteen minutes. Then we can go on down to the slop-shop for some din-din. You et yet?"

"No." Masterson laughed loudly as if something one of them said had been funny.

"Well, *all right* then. See you soon then, ol' buddy." Moke turned to go back to his room, but Masterson said something else he couldn't hear, which sounded like, "I guess you're the serious type."

"What's that?" Moke said.

"I said, 'My roommate's not here right now.' But you'll meet the bastard soon enough. He's a nigger."

"Oh."

"Isn't that a pisser!"

At dinner Moke learned that Masterson was also a pre-med major—in fact, Masterson's father, he said, was an alumnus of the Med School—and Masterson said usually two-thirds of the freshman class "started out" in pre-med and they had to "wash 'em out early" to get the class down to a reasonable size. Masterson had already bought one of the Duke University T-shirts, with blue piping around the sleeves, and every time he took a forkful of peas or moved his arms the incredible bulk of his biceps and pectorals strained at the cloth.

Masterson said weight-lifting was about the best exercise there was because you could get more accomplished in a shorter time and really increase your strength and improve your definition. Masterson kept five hundred pounds of Joe-Weider-brand barbells in his room and said he lifted weights for two hours every day, which wasn't hard to believe.

Masterson said he couldn't figure out why they had given *him* "a jungle bunny" for a roommate. But he guessed, as long as the bastard kept to his own side of the room and didn't try to borrow his hair oil, he wasn't going to make a big issue out of it. This, too, was funny, for some reason.

Moke decided that Masterson was a hardcore bigot. He had heard about such people, but as the son of two high-school teachers living in a sheltered suburb in the Midwest, he had never encountered one in such a pure form. He wasn't certain what he should do. He felt called upon to state a position or challenge Masterson in some way. He imagined what might happen if he suddenly raised up and threw the heavy table, spilling the dishes, platters, and catsup bottle into Masterson's lap, like an angry gambler who knows he's caught someone cheating at poker on one of the late-late movies.

"Maybe you'll like him better after you get to know him," Moke suggested. "Give him a chance, for heaven's sake. Think how he must feel."

"Yeah, you're right," Masterson said. "He may not even *be* a nigger, for all I know. Maybe he's just got a fantastic suntan!" He laughed uproariously and slapped the tabletop.

In fact, Masterson's roommate was not a Negro. His name was Norman Adujabi, and he was a helplessly shy, somber boy with dark almond eyes, olive skin, and a slightly foreign, Mideastern look, whose boney knuckles were always straining around the handle of an enormous briefcase that seemed too immense and weighty for his slender body. Norman was the only other one who ever stayed regularly after the 4:30 zoology bell or came back to the lab after dinner. He was also the only other one who ever got up regularly by 6 A.M. and took himself to the freshman lounge to watch the special chemistry program on educational TV recommended by Dr. Portier.

When he encountered Moke for their early morning vigils, he seldom spoke but would smile politely and prepare his clipboard and expensive-looking pen for the onslaught of information from the TV. Whoever arrived first, by tacit agreement, got the set warmed up and the chairs arranged. The two of them seated there morning after morning—in the deserted lounge with its baronial splendor in red leather chairs with deluxe rivets before the flicker of the television and the steady gray early morning light from the high Gothic casements—cemented a relationship. Norman's usually stolid features would always bend into a shy smile of recognition and greeting if he passed Moke coming out of the Chem Building later in the day, lunging to pull his gargantuan briefcase past the doorjamb before the heavy door swung shut upon it or, later yet, in zoology lab again, where Norman worked methodically on numerous careful drawings of all their assigned dissections. Norman became a kind of standard freshman year, for Moke to measure himself against. Above all, he was determined not to fail from sheer laziness, and he knew that if he worked as hard and as earnestly as Norman was working, he could work no harder.

Julie wrote to say she was lonely and morose and wished she could see him as soon as possible. She speculated that marriage before their senior year might be feasible after all, if she could graduate in three years and get a job; or possibly she could transfer to Duke and study to become an X-ray technician or something practical.

The zoology-comparative anatomy lab was an amazing and horrifying place. Arranged in old oak-lined glass cases around the perimeter were specimens of snakes and internal organs and insects of hideous proportions, even the embalmed spiral of a sixty-foot-long human tapeworm in one corner. On top of the cases were perched, most prominently, the complete reassembled skeleton of a mountain goat and various fossil skulls and, elsewhere, skeletons of smaller animals, mostly mammals. Wall charts on two walls displayed gigantic enlargements of hydra and paramecia and jellyfish and cross-sections of the human eyeball with all its parts labeled.

The eyeball looked faintly bloodshot, and when Moke looked up from his work he frequently stared at it. It made him think of all the other eyes he had studied so far in zoology: the eye of his dogfish shark, carefully dissected from the peeled chondrocranium on the tip of a scalpel, lovely and transparent as a marble, precious vitreous fluids tenuously immured in a delicate spherical membrane one-cell deep; the eye of the honey bee that perceives ultraviolet as a color in nature and the sky as the undersurface of a tessellated dome, checkerboard squares of gray and white and black shifting with the sun like stars in a planetarium, a built-in sextant; or the compound eyes of the ordinary housefly that must see the world as if through twin kaleidoscopes. Who was to say how the world actually looked?

Moke continued to work late in the zoology lab, occasionally imagining his own eyes growing as bulbous and bloodshot as the one on the wall-chart.

Though it was still early in the semester, Moke's professor in Religion/Philosophy 101 assigned a topic for the final exam. It was to be a single question upon which they were to come prepared to write for three hours without notes. The question was: What is life? A collective groan went up from the class, but Moke thought he liked the idea. The more he considered it, the better he liked it. They would have plenty of time to prepare; there would be no anxiety about having to regurgitate segments of the textbook they had already covered. No ridiculous cramming. He could just systematically research the question when he had time and think about it in the meantime. And what a question! *What is life?* Perfect. This was what he had come to college to think about, the ultimate questions. This was why he was so interested in medicine, after all, wasn't it? Because it had to do with life-and-death issues.

His zoology textbook itself, he found, which was entitled *Life,* discussed the question of *What is life?* but only in terms of biological processes. Surely a religion/philosophy professor would not be satisfied with a merely physical or mechanistic definition, and it did not satisfy Moke either. *The living organism maintains itself, grows, and reproduces its own likeness.* But to what purpose? Why should it bother?

Searching through the library stacks for a better answer to his question, Moke began to encounter varieties of information, speculation, dogma, and inquiry he had not known existed. He began to read eclectically and, as time leaked away, a little desperately: *Philosophic Classics: Bacon to Kant, Philosophy Made Simple* (covertly), *What Is Existentialism?, Leviathan, The Humanity of Man, The Meaning of Meaning, Beyond Good and Evil, Lady Chatterly's Lover, Civilization and Its Discontents.* He discovered he was part of something called "the human condition."

Dr. Vernon returned the lab tests on Thursday. He was a compact, formal, muscular little man who wore navy three-piece suits, gestured impressively with his broad, short-fingered hands, and was almost completely bald. The lab tests were notoriously difficult. Zoology 101 was notoriously difficult. Masterson had been right, he guessed. They were trying to weed out the lightweights.

When Moke saw the 69 on his paper, his heart grew weak. He folded the quiz quickly away into his briefcase, his ears turning hot. If he failed zoology, his life would be over—his image of himself, his chances for medical school, everything. God, a 69, and he thought he had done reasonably well. He tried to concentrate on Dr. Vernon's instructions for the lab assignment on chick embryos. With each point made, Dr. Vernon pounded his square-tipped forefinger rhythmically into his left palm for emphasis. As soon as the brief lecture was over and the class had started to work on the dissections, Moke went up to the blackboard and stood around until Dr. Vernon was free. "Could I talk to you . . . privately, I mean?" Moke said.

"About the test?"

"Yes." Vernon walked with him into one of the nearby supply rooms and shut the door. The space was lined with jars and reeked of formaldehyde and embalming fluid. It seemed a little embarrassing to be suddenly shut off from the others with this intense, hawk-like little man, who stared at him sharply and waited for Moke to speak. "I was wondering if I might do something extra to make up for the quiz," Moke said. "I can't believe I did so poorly."

"We don't keep you busy enough, is that it, Mr. Galenaille?"

"I've been working on it very hard, I really have. I wouldn't want any special treatment, but I know I can do better than I did. I think I just need more work . . . or . . ." He felt his eyes begin to cloud over slightly, irrationally, a sensation of self-pity he had not felt so strongly since childhood. He was furious with himself.

"That's all right, Mr. Galenaille. You needn't worry yet. In fact, your score was twenty points higher than anyone else in the section. I doubt if you need any more work for the moment, but if I detect later on in the semester that you seem to be running out of things to do, I'll be certain to let you know." He clapped Moke manfully on the back and ushered him back into the laboratory.

As the semester picked up momentum and they all began to feel swamped under the load of work, Masterson still spent hours clanging around his room with his weights. The apparatus took up so much floor space that he had, more or less, driven Norman into the least desirable third of their room. As Moke passed the open door of Normans'-and-

Masterson's room in his hectic comings and goings, he would often see Norman huddled in his corner, his determined features focused above the cone of light from his study lamp and his hands clamped over his ears. Eventually, Norman took to wearing a pair of earmuffs to block out Masterson's constant huffing and crashing and inane monologue.

Masterson had quickly learned to wear the ubiquitous light beige London Fog windbreakers and chinos and no socks with his penny loafers and became adept at frisbee. He oddly persisted in pretending that Norman was black and in baiting him with racist insults. Moke never responded to these gibes but was made so uncomfortable by them that he imagined Masterson did it partly to insult him as well. Later on Masterson grew somewhat friendlier and referred to Norman in all conversations as Nerman-the-Herman. Several others on the hall, mistaking Masterson's maliciousness for wit, or actually mistaking the name, started referring to poor, serious, dignified Norman as Nerman. "How ya doin', Nerman!" "See yaroun', Nerman."

Then one day between Thanksgiving and Christmas, Norman was abruptly absent from the morning TV session. Moke was mildly pleased at first, thinking he had outlasted even solid Norman and taking this as evidence of his own virtue. But he was vaguely uneasy; he kept expecting Norman to come in late, excusing himself for his tardiness, and to start right to work, copying formulas as before. The next day Norman's absence began to seem more permanent and alarming. Norman wasn't the sort of person to give up so easily. Moke frankly missed his companionship. He found himself growing drowsy and paying little attention to the program and worrying about Norman. It seemed pointless to get up at such an ungodly hour if not even Norman was there to witness his act of sacrifice. He decided to stop coming. Norman was absent from zoology lab, too, and from the hall.

The following Friday he chanced to eat lunch at a table where Masterson was holding forth. Masterson had a black eye and a bruised-looking purple mark on the side of his face. Moke wasn't thinking about Norman at the time, but Masterson brought it up: "You hear what happened between me and Nerman?" he said. The way Masterson told it, Masterson had been lifting weights, clanging around the room as usual, and was just stooping over to try to clean-and-jerk 280 pounds, a new personal record if he had only done it, when Norman suddenly sneaked up behind him clutching a ten-pound dumbbell weight and (for no reason at all) brained him on the side of the head. "I didn't know I was livin' in the same room with a homicidal fuckin' maniac!" Masterson said. Masterson slipped to his knees but quickly recovered himself, shook his head two or three times like a slightly stunned wounded animal, and went after Norman roaring and cursing and swinging. He caught Norman with a shot that "pulverized" Norman's cheekbone and then he chased him around the room and up and down the halls and finally treed him in the quad where Norman climbed to the shaky top branches and "squealed and carried on until the dean showed up and then the little men in the white coats came and carried the son of a bitch away to the looney bin, I swear to God," and Masterson pounded the table with his sense of this evidence of divine justice. "And now I've got that whole gorgeous double *awll* to myself!" he added.

Whether or not Norman was in the looney bin, he had certainly been absent from his usual classes and schedule, and Moke continued to wonder about him. One night in the deserted lab while he was returning his microscope to its cabinet, Moke was struck by the impulse to check Norman's cabinet to see if it had ever been cleared out. Sure enough, the lock was missing and there was no microscope—it was a university microscope; the lab assistant must have taken it back to the supply room. Curiously, Moke opened each of the little wooden drawers in the cabinet, hoping for some evidence that Norman had once used this particular locker. In one of the drawers, he found something that made his hair stand on end. It was a cylindrical plastic vial containing clear formaldehyde, and floating in the formaldehyde like a piece of half-chewed pork chop was the perfectly dissected brain of a frog. They had not worked at all on frogs' brains. Norman must have dissected it on his own. He never saw Norman Adujabi again.

That week he received a letter from Julie Greenway informing him that she had had four dates with boys from Amherst, one of whom drove a black MG, that her grades were going to pot, and that she thought their relationship was in danger of becoming too serious, on the one hand, and too difficult to maintain, on the other, "outside the social context in which it started." She recommended a cooling-off period during which they would write less frequently and think about each other less often. Moke drank half-a-bottle of Beaujolais, mailed back her ring special delivery, burned her picture and all her letters, and felt miserable—even sick—for days on end, as if a close friend had died.

It was around this time that Moke started lifting weights. He ordered five hundred pounds of Joe-Weider-brand iron—dumbbells, barbells, collars, wrenches, a "Samson twister" for "putting knife-sharp definition in arm, chest, and shoulder muscles," and a subscription to *Muscle Builder* magazine. When the shipment arrived at the university post office, it took him six trips to lug the equipment back to his room. Before he did, he made sure Masterson was nowhere to be found and that the hall was deserted. He didn't want any extraneous comments from *any*body. What he did in his room was his business.

He started working out with a vengeance, reading and studying the muscle magazines. He concocted a powerful porridge of wheat germ, Special K, and brewer's yeast that he consumed in gigantic portions at bedtime after his work-outs. Only last year Julie Greenway's mother had referred to him as "skinny Moke," not exactly to his face but to Julie's; and Julie hadn't hesitated to pass on the insult. Moke ruminated about this morosely as he sweated through his routines, then frequently took out the tape measure and measured his biceps, his forearms, his chest normal, his chest expanded, his thighs and calves—to see if he had gained any new bulk. He gave himself burning-hot sunlamp treatments in the nude, screwing the conical bulb into his study-lamp socket.

In Comparative Anatomy lab, the dissections moved speedily along from the dogfish shark to their large project—the house cat. His specimen, skinned and swollen from the embalming tank, was as big as a cocker spaniel and the most hideous beast he had ever seen or imagined. Each lab day he had to fish for it by plunging his arm up to his bicep in cold formaldehyde and pulling up plastic bags full of dead cats until he could locate the one with his name on it. He began to spend so many hours with this same horrendous cat, picking away at its organs, that he could eventually identify it by the shape alone, even inside its bag. Breathing the stench of it for three hours at a sitting left him with whanging headaches. His attitude toward the cat changed from contempt and loathing to guilt (at the desecration he was forced to enact), admiration, and a kind of friendliness verging on tenderness.

His empty mailbox. His palms sweating in chemistry class or so icy cold he would press them between his thighs and the curved wooden seat until the circulation was cut off and he would have to shake them to write again, watching his white knuckles furiously inscribing formulas page after page.

It rained for a week. Walking from chem lab and zoology-comparative anatomy lab to the post office to his room, dodging the hoards on the broad, uneven flagstone sidewalks, there was no way to keep from splashing water in your sock. The imposing neo-Gothic edifice blotted out all horizons, all sunsets. Two more weeks went by and still no reply from Julie. That was finished. Could she have lost his address? Moke decided to grow a beard. He would never shave again. He would take on the look of some returning Arctic explorer or some bushy disciple of Sigmund Freud.

Late at night, as he studied quietly in his room, drunken fraternity goons rode by in convertibles and yelled: "Hit dem books, frosh! Hit dem books, you muthas!"

He began taking long late-night walks to look at the girly magazines at one downtown drugs-and-sundries and spent sometimes forty-five minutes flipping through the pages before buying—first hoping to find a picture resembling Julie, finally settling on the loveliest women available—testing his powers of discrimination on the smallest details—then rushing back to his room and masturbating with pounding heart and hand. How he loved women. He loved them in every posture, in every light. He loved every ridiculous thing they did in the magazines and he never tired of their antics. They were always willing, always available, always his alone.

One night as he was walking along in the shadow of a dark factory, a dusty overloaded car rattled past and some nut yelled, "Hey, Castro, go back to Cuba!" and hit him hard in the back with a half-empty beer can.

Only later on would he realize that his confusion and increasing frustration over the question *What is life?* were partly the result of his unconsciously extending the question to include, too intimately, What is *the purpose* of life? and *What is the purpose of MY life?* But the overriding question *What is life?* began to seem utterly burdensome to him. He would prepare his other work, his German translations, his calculus, zoology, and chemistry exercises—everything straightforward and neat—and then he would still have this monumental conundrum to face, which began to seem more puzzling and immense than the riddle of the Sphinx. What *is* life? What is *life*? It began to seem either sheer nonsense or the most important question he had ever asked.

Next to his desk in the library was a botany section containing, to his amazement, *The Weeds of North Carolina* in seventeen volumes; and this workman-like little series bound in light-green boards began to symbolize the absurdity of existence, the uselessness of all human effort, and the futility of his ever knowing enough to answer *the big question* on his philosophy final. To *think* that someone probably devoted his entire life to classifying weeds, and to think that weeds would grow in such profusion that it would take seventeen volumes just to identify the ones in North Carolina!

"Life in the state of nature," he read, "is solitary, poor, nasty, brutish, and short." But wouldn't the case be worse, he thought, if it were nasty, brutish, and *long*? Sometimes he felt as if he might be near the edge of a breakthrough, some ultimate postulate he could not quite comprehend or articulate. If only he could . . . dig deeper, have more time to prepare . . . *think*.

It occurred to him during December that maybe medical school wasn't the answer. That had been Julie's idea anyway. Maybe Duke wasn't the answer. Maybe he needed to "find" himself first. Sometimes he could see himself just hitchhiking West, working his way, maybe, picking grapes for a few weeks in some small mountain town in California, just stepping aboard any bus that happened along, not knowing where it was going or where he was ending up.

Rain dripped past the lab windows all afternoon, forming in puddles on the walks and spilling out into the bright grass. Students coming out of the Chem Building across the quad snapped out black pushbutton umbrellas or ran like madmen toward the library. When the bell rang at four-thirty, the doors downstairs began thumping and everyone left the lab except him.

Moke squeezed the bulge the small bottle of sperm made through his shirtpocket and laid a clean slide directly in front of him on the desk. He felt a little like a mad scientist who was about to inject himself with a disease in order to try to discover its cure. (He was going to have one helluva time explaining where he got this stuff if somebody caught him and wanted to know what he was doing.) Quickly he slipped the bottle out, uncapped it, poured a little of the sperm onto the slide and placed a cover glass on it, recapped the bottle with lightning speed and jammed it back into his pocket. He fastened the slide to the microscope and focused in, keeping both eyes open (as he had learned), his left eye over the eyepiece. The field sharpened, sharpened, and there they were, unbelievable zillions of them! Even after about seventeen hours most of them were still alive and eager! Well, there were a few dead ones, yes. *But, my God, look at them! They have different-length flagella! They are so different from one another! Live creatures out of my own body! My God, who would ever believe such a thing!*

It was the first morning of final-exam week and Moke went down to the head with his soap dish, washrag and towel over his arm, toothbrush, Crest, hairbrush, and scissors—feeling like a monk with begging bowl, ascetic and worn out—and stepped into line with Masterson, Clark, Gallagher, and Hamilton in front of the big row of mirrors and lavatories. Steam hovered near the ceiling over the shower stalls and odors of Old Spice and Listerine mingled with the harsh laundry-soap pungence of their towels and the stench of Masterson's hair concoction. Masterson had his elbows positioned carefully above his head, raking and shaping his miserable mop with an Ace comb into his idea of debonair collegiate insouciance. Moke washed his face and started to brush and clip at his beard.

"Why in the world do you *have* that thing?" Masterson said. "Why don't you *shave*?"

"I don't think it's any business of yours what I do," Moke said. Gallagher, who was busily shaving on Masterson's left, said, "Yeah!" Gallagher was in Moke's chemistry section and was his wrestling partner in gym, due to sheer alphabetical proximity, even though outweighing Moke by seventy pounds. Gallagher had received offers of football scholarships from forty schools and was considered a celebrity.

"It may not be my business," Masterson said, "but I still have to look at the rancid thing every day. It looks like some kind of goddamned cabbage growing out of your cheeks." He winked in Gallagher's direction, evidently thinking this sort of kidding would appeal to Gallagher's sense of the rightness of things.

"Your whole *head* looks like a goddamned cabbage to me," Moke said.

"Watch it, you fucking Commie, or I'll use your face for a toilet swab."

Moke's right arm swung like heavy rubber around Masterson's porcine neck and Masterson's uplifted comb fell away and glanced off the rim of the lavatory. Moke forced Masterson's huge off-balance bulk across the room and slammed him hard against the marble shower stall.

"Ouch," Masterson said. "Now you've done it." His face showed utter astonishment. Someone grabbed Moke's arm from the rear and prevented it from punching Masterson's scowling mouth.

"I'm not Norman!" Moke yelled. "So don't think you can push me around!" Two of them were restraining Masterson, too, who was rubbing the back of his head and not trying to pull loose.

"You're asking for it, Santa Claus," Masterson said. "You're asking for a knuckle sandwich, and you're gonna get it."

"From you and who else?"

"All right, you guys," Gallagher yelled, "cut it out!"

"As soon as I put Galenaille's head in the toilet," Masterson said, starting to reach out with his ape-like arms.

"Cool it, Masterson," Gallagher said. Masterson squirmed and fought, and the next thing Moke knew Clark and Gallagher were forcing

Masterson into the toilet stall and Masterson was screaming, "Nooo, noooo!" and Gallagher was saying, "Kneel down, you bastard, before I break your arm," and then slowly squeezing Masterson's bullet-like head toward the bowl and saying, "Take a drink, Queerbait. *You heard me, drink it!* And then you can sit up and apologize like a good boy."

Moke had spent more time and effort preparing for *What is life?* than on any other single subject, but when he came to the examination room that morning, edged into the hardbacked seat, and stared at the first page of the bluebook, something froze within him. The lines of the booklet seemed too widely spaced. *What is life?* he wrote. But his hand would not make the necessary motions across the page to fill in any further lines. Other students seated nearby were already scribbling furiously. *What could they be saying?* The feat of moving a pen across a page at such speed seemed as absurd, as impossible, as frogs juggling beachballs. His hands were like ice. The image of Masterson with his head bowed toward the toilet bowl flashed through his mind. The fact was that in three months of struggling and digging he had not succeeded in discovering any satisfactory answer to the question *What is life?* His present position was somewhere between a sort of humanist-agnostic-existentialist and a pantheistic hedonist.

Spermatozoa dancing in a field of light—he wrote—*are they conscious? Can they feel? What can they know of the world beyond themselves, of their creator, or their ultimate destination? One in millions will survive until the end of the journey, to the egg gleaming larger and more radiant than the Taj Mahal at the end of the Fallopian tube. With what yearning does that single potent spermatozoan swim leapingly toward this awesome and gigantic pearl while his fellows fall away and drop on every side, their short lives forever spent. And what unique message does he whisper to her in order to gain entrance to her palace within? Suddenly, he sees, the walls recede—he is bathed in light as if entering the sun itself in a chariot drawn by golden stallions . . . .*

He received A's in all his pre-med subjects and a C in religion/philosophy.

Julie Greenway never did write back. She transferred from Smith to Northwestern, he heard, to be closer to home and to her new boyfriend, who was going to graduate school there, studying international trade. Two years later she married him and four months after that she went to sleep and quietly died under anesthesia during an unsuccessful Caesarean section operation in Chicago. Moke, then in graduate school himself—in philosophy—found this news difficult to believe. He could not imagine Julie Greenway inside a coffin in the ground, her body surrounded by white satin, not breathing, not moving, roots slowing pressing against the box, forcing it apart. It gave him nightmares for years afterwards.

Eventually, Moke Galenaille was to become a teacher of the humanities at a little known liberal arts college in the Midwest. He was inquisitive, reliable, and fair-minded with his students—only occasionally dull—and he believed all his life in the importance of asking the ultimate questions. He came to be well liked, even by his colleagues, though more for his passionate enthusiasm, innocent nature, and interest in others than for his discernment or skill.

Roth's Deadman

The deadman's head was rotated slightly toward the window; and the desultory afternoon, the sun hard on the trees beside the parking lot and the sprinklers working in the grass, encroached upon the room in unbroken vividness and multiformity. The plastic intravenous tube was still taped at the ankle, the swollen yellow ankle, yellow and swollen as the face and neck of the man, fifty-four years old according to his wristband, now dead, admitted three days previously, alive upon arrival, two days in a coma, and gone now ten minutes before Roth could get there to see it happen.

The chart in the nurse's station said the deadman in 117 was J. B. Houk; business executive; L. R. Downing, Inc.; divorced, two children; possibly alcoholic.

Roth, the new orderly, had often come to stand quietly behind the curtain and watch the phenomenon of J. B. Houk before he died. Roth would stand over the bed and wonder what kind of man J. B. Houk was. The barrel chest of the man heaved irregularly, and his body always appeared to be sucking dextrose from the intravenous tube, drawing in the liquid with ruthless energy. There was something vaguely brutal or unscrupulous in the face, lines about the mouth fixed through time into an automatic hypocritical grimace of benevolence displayed for some selfish end. The hair was pure white above the jaundiced face—some might have called him a distinguished-looking man—and the eyes had been blue, very light blue and surprisingly transparent when Roth first saw them, before J. B. Houk closed his eyes that second day and allowed his body to labor on unburdened by consciousness.

Ray was already stripping clothes out of the closet and folding them up at the foot of the bed. "What should I do?" Roth said.

"I was waiting till you got here to do the body," Ray said. He brought a small suitcase out of the closet and a scarlet-patterned bathrobe on a hanger and placed the clothes he had finished folding into the suitcase, then the bathrobe, exposing the bald spot in his flattop as he bent down. "We'll have to take care of all these belongings," Ray said, pointing to the nightstand. "I'm supposed to show you how to finish him up so you can do it yourself next time."

"Will we have to take him downstairs?"

"No, Scobie's will be here in a few minutes. They'll take care of him. We don't usually store them here at the hospital." Roth visualized the door to the morgue, identical to the other doors he passed every afternoon on the basement floor after punching his timecard, except for the black lettering on it (he might have expected that kind of door to be made of stone or heavy metal).

Ray handed him a paper bag, and Roth went to the nightstand and opened the drawer. Inside was a pair of glasses without a case, a gold wristwatch, wallet, set of car keys, ballpoint pen, four or five packs of matches from a cocktail joint, two large twenty-five-cent cigars, and a circular indexed marker for locating appropriate Biblical passages "when in doubt," "when laden with temptation," "when suffering ill health," etc. Roth placed the articles carefully in the open bag like packed groceries. In the cabinet section of the nightstand was a Gideon's Bible and a dog-eared pile of magazines, a blur of red-margined covers with words like "consumer" and "world" on them—filled with graphs, statistics, and pictures of other businessmen. Roth scooped them up and laid them in the open suitcase with the folded paper bag.

"Miss Trigg said to be sure not to disturb Mr. Tilney," Ray whispered. "He's liable to have another cardiac." Roth reached back and pulled the curtain taut that separated the two beds in the room, wondering for a moment what the frightened unknown little man who lay between them and the door might be thinking.

"He's been playing possum, I think," Roth whispered. The bedsprings squeaked at this and Ray chuckled nervously.

"Thinks it might be a bad omen. They're likely to start going three-at-a-time, you know." Roth shrugged.

"Now," Ray said, "the first thing you do is remove any dentures he might have, close his mouth so his jaw won't freeze open, and get his head straight on the pillow, nose up—otherwise you might get a blue cheek."

"Right."

"You can imagine how a blue cheek would go over with the funeral home." Ray quickly inserted his fingers in the half-opened mouth, pushed the tongue back, brought his hands out again almost immediately, and closed the jaw with his palm. Then he gripped the head above the hairline and turned it counterclockwise away from the window. The head stayed where he put it.

"He hasn't got any false teeth."

"Good."

"Notice how I was careful not to touch the skin except where I had to. Wherever you touch him, that part's going to turn color, so you've got to be careful."

"How will they get this yellow out of him? He seems pretty discolored already."

"They have ways. Yellow's easier than blue, and yellow's not our fault. They'll have him laid out looking like the picture of health. Don't worry. He'll be the healthiest-looking man at the funeral."

"Shouldn't we get this intravenous out?" Ray nodded.

"It doesn't matter much if you touch him there because nobody sees that." Ray quickly unraveled the bandage at the ankle and was extracting the needle. Roth unhooked the dextrose bottle to give him slack, scrutinizing the greenish underwater effigy of his face reflected from the glass container, his head weirdly suspended above the starched hospital shirt.

Just then Roth heard a sound of rubber-soled shoes shrieking on the vinyl of the outer hall. The door of the room across the hall was slightly ajar, but nothing was visible but the door itself, surrounded by the immaculate tile walls of the corridor. Then Miss Trigg, the head nurse, came shrieking through the door frame. He and Ray started like grave robbers.

"The family's here to visit," she said. "Have you got him ready? Dr. Shantril hasn't told them yet. He's on his way down."

A brown-haired woman appeared in the hallway, and Miss Trigg blushed and turned to look at the body. The suitcase was still lying open next to it on the bed, and the bony feet and ankles, bruised and purple from the intravenous, were sticking out where the sheet was pulled up. The body was uncovered above the waist.

"He's not quite ready yet," Ray said.

Roth's hand was gripping the iron barrel of the intravenous rack. He could see the woman pause in the doorway and speak to someone out of sight. Miss Trigg yanked the sheet, covering the toes, and quickly tucked it in across the bottom. Ray was reaching toward the suitcase, still clutching the ankle bandage, when Roth saw the woman start to move.

"She's coming in," Roth said.

"I'm sorry," Miss Trigg said, partially blocking the woman at the foot of Mr. Tilney's bed, "you'll have to wait until the doctor arrives." Two girls, one about twelve, one about sixteen, had come in behind the woman. They looked at Miss Trigg expectantly.

"Has there been any change?" the woman said. The sixteen-year-old girl was watching Roth as he wheeled the intravenous rack against the wall. She had brown fluffy hair down to her shoulders. Ray brought out the closed suitcase and crossed behind Miss Trigg and laid it on the chair. Miss Trigg seemed to be at a loss for words. The older girl gave her a frightened look and suddenly stepped around her and planted herself beside the deadman's bed. She seemed to rise up on the balls of her feet.

"The doctor should be here any minute, Mrs. Houk," Miss Trigg said. "I'm sorry." They were all looking at the body now.

The woman's expression was haggard, resigned, immediately resigned, faintly disgusted. "I'll be all right," she said. Then the older girl threw herself upon the swollen, yellow man and desperately kissed the rigid face. Her back heaved up and down.

"Oh, Daddy," she sobbed. "Oh, Daddy, Daddy."

Beautiful Vases

A new student—Stephanie Adams—stopped by Professor O'Reilly's office that day, and what she wanted him to do was preposterous. She was a striking, blond-haired girl with large eyes, a small, rather prim mouth, and a bright, nervous manner. What she hoped to persuade him to do would ordinarily have been easy to provide: a recommendation for a summer program, an internship, to do newspaper work in New York. However, she had not yet taken any of his courses. In fact, he had never seen her before in his life.

Still, she expected him to recommend her, to do this "great favor" for her in spite of the unusual circumstances, because she was certain that, without his help, she would have no chance of being accepted. She *would* take the necessary courses from him the following semester, she promised. He *would* find out that she was a talented writer upon whom a strong recommendation had not been wasted.

The problem was that she had decided only last week that her life's work was to be as a journalist. She had been rushing around trying to find out if there was still time to cram in the necessary courses and graduate on time, and, luckily, she found she could just manage it. She sighed and touched her hair and gave him a supplicating look. But the internship was truly indispensable. She would do anything to convince him, absolutely anything.

Ordinarily, O'Reilly would have given her an apologetic no, but partly because of her hopefulness and energy, and partly because he didn't want to squelch her enthusiasm if she was, in fact, going to become a new major, he agreed to read the two papers she had brought along as examples of her work and let her know the next day if he could, in good conscience, write to the newspaper people in her behalf.

"Oh, wonderful," she cooed. "I just had a feeling you would understand. I'm so psyched!"

The papers, which he went over at home that night after dinner, were a disappointment. They had been submitted for an education course and were full of social science jargon, poorly phrased. They were not only badly written but carelessly punctuated. The education professor had given her an A- on one of them and had written a number of fatuous, irrelevant remarks in the margins in red pencil. He shook his head in disbelief and tried to think of a tactful way to decline her request.

But when she came to his office the next day, she was wearing a lemon yellow sweater in some very soft fiber, mohair or cashmere, and her light blond hair falling across her shoulders reminded him of an engraving he had seen of some classical heroine, Penelope or Andromeda. She was beautiful. She was wearing a wool skirt and expensive-looking toeless pumps with her elegant, perfectly painted toes just visible in a bright stylish enamel. She seemed older and looked extremely professional. She seemed to have dressed up expressly for the occasion, in fact, as if she were already a professional journalist. She was so certain that her papers were marvelous, so certain that he would now be eager to perform his necessary role in the launching of her embryonic career, that instead of finding the words to say no to her, he found himself agreeing to write a letter.

He didn't want her to get her hopes up too high, he said, but he would do his best under the circumstances. He wanted her to realize that she would be competing against students from other schools who had had extensive course work and possibly several years of experience writing for campus newspapers, but all that seemed to matter to her was that she had gained his consent—that was all she could hope for, she said, under the circumstances—and she was delighted.

Later, faced with the chore of writing the actual letter, which would have to be one lie after another, he was ashamed of himself. He knew he should never have agreed to such a thing. It took him the better part of an afternoon, sweating away and feeling like a fool; and the way he accomplished it, finally, was to write the recommendation as if he were fondly remembering one of his brightest students, saying all the necessary things.

As he explained in his letter to the Dean: When the invitation from Brockton College came in the mail, he had been working on ideas for Stephanie Adams' Independent Study project. . . . The invitation came from a young assistant professor at Brockton, Mary Fowler, whom he had met once, briefly, at a journalism convention and who, somewhat mistakenly, had the notion that he was one of the powers in the field. He was flattered, of course, and could use the extra money offered by the honorarium, but he didn't travel often these days to give lectures. This school was a five- or six-hour drive, too far, he thought, for a comfortable trip. He hadn't taken any long drives since his wife had died. He was about to write a letter turning down the speaking date when he had a brainstorm: it occurred to him that here might be a novel way to give Stephanie Adams some practical experience for her Independent Study project.

His proposal, which he explained to Stephanie, was that she could come along as his assistant. She would photograph and tape record the lecture and attempt to "cover" the event as if she were on assignment for a real newspaper or magazine. This would give her an opportunity to find out if she liked the sort of work that a reporter was called upon to do. She could write it up as one of her assignments for his Independent Study course, and he would also be able to pay her a small sum for her trouble from a budget he had available for student assistants. Her presence would make the drive down less tedious for him. Stephanie seemed delighted by the offer and said she thought she could "really get into" a trip like that, so he went ahead and accepted the speaking date for mid-February.

Thinking about it later, he remembered that from the moment he picked her up at her dorm on the day of the trip to Brockton, she seemed in a sullen mood. The collar of her beige coat was turned up against the wind, and she couldn't quite manage a smile when he greeted her. He held open the passenger's door for her and then carefully tucked her suitcase into the trunk beside his briefcase and overnighter and slammed the lid and got in. "We're off," he said. The sky was overcast, but he was looking forward to the trip and feeling cheerful, even exuberant. He had no idea why she was so down-in-the-mouth—maybe a falling out with her boyfriend or roommate or maybe just the weather, who could tell? Girls her age were sometimes unpredictably moody.

Often, in the past, when his wife was still alive, he could coax her out of a depression by a persistent display of kidding and sympathy and his own good spirits. But, in spite of his joviality and best efforts at good humor over the next several hours, Stephanie did not respond. If anything, she clammed up all the more, often staring out the side window so that when he glanced over at her all he could see was the back of her blond head, with its perfect part and the elegant folds of hair swooping down across her shoulders. He began to wonder if he had done something to offend her, but, for the life of him, he could not imagine what it might be.

She was an amazingly attractive girl, beautiful really, according to all the customary definitions. He had a harder time knowing now whether girls of her age were beautiful or not. Some of them who seemed beautiful to him at first, on the first day in class, for instance, later began to seem quite ordinary; and he realized that they were probably just young and fresh-faced and did not seem particularly beautiful to their peers, and might, in fact, be unpopular and unappreciated and—simply not beautiful.

The truth of the matter was that he was forty-eight and his wife had died only last year. He noticed that Stephanie Adams was an attractive girl, of course. But she was his student, someone he scarcely knew outside of a classroom-and-office situation, and she was so young, impossible for him to take seriously at his age. She was so nearly a child, had so recently been merely a child; she was scarcely formed, immature, a blank slate. O'Reilly felt he was perfectly safe from so transient a factor as beauty. He had already navigated in those waters and crossed the bar into respectable middle age.

So many of the young women he taught, like Stephanie Adams, were attractive, receptive, malleable—they were at the most nubile of ages. He was not stupid or numb, and he appreciated their inherent attractiveness, but always, abstractly, as if from a great distance, as one might appreciate a collection of beautiful vases. He had once seen a Picasso exhibit in Boston, in fact, that included some enormous, lifesize vases shaped like women's bodies and conceived with Picasso's great licentious craftiness and style. From a distance, they resembled statues of sensuous women. It was only on closer inspection that one could see they were actually just huge droll vases, capable of holding a quantity of flower stalks or reeds or umbrellas, and that, because they were museum pieces, they were, of course, empty.

While once, within recent memory, he had identified quite closely with his students, now they seemed members of some alien tribe or species, whose arrogance and cheerfulness and intense, obvious needs often seemed absurd, and whose beauty was akin to pottery or the exotic markings of some nearly extinct strain of birdlife one might read about in *National Geographic,* occasionally astonishing but so universal within the genotype as to be for the most part unremarkable. In his occupation, professors kept getting older and older, but students stayed the same age. The illusion was that his clients were getting younger and younger, as if he were gazing at them through the wrong end of a telescope.

He remembered his wife very clearly. He had lived under the same roof with her for twenty years, and he had watched her change from the young, lovely girl he had married into a handsome woman of middle age, and he had watched her die, and he had never once regretted marrying her. That was true—he never had—in spite of the usual tiffs and misunderstandings, the usual adjustments. Surely that was exceptional. He could see her lying on the couch in the limp, delicate way she did at the end, looking so incredibly sad and resigned. He would come up to her and take her face in his hands and pat her cheeks softly and pretend to kiss her nose, and he could see her eyes turning up at the corners, cutting through the desolate expression that had been there the moment before. To press her body against his felt like touching some angelic power of healing, something nearly divine, yet she could not heal herself and he could not heal her— no one could. She was taken from him, and he would never be the same again. He knew that as surely as he knew anything in the world.

Now, for a few minutes, for some reason he could not put his finger on, this girl, Stephanie Adams, reminded him of his wife, and he felt unreasonably happy because of it. Of course, he knew it was only an illusion. There was scarcely any resemblance at all, nothing to support the momentary elation. When they finally pulled up to the Holiday Inn in Brockton, his own emotional state was beginning to slide.

The faculty sponsor for his appearance, Mary Fowler, was supposed to be ready to meet them at the Holiday Inn upon arrival, provide a schedule and a tour of campus, and see to Ms. Adams' dormitory accommodations. O'Reilly called the number he had been given from the lobby phone but received no answer. After several tries with no better luck, he decided to check in and try again from his room. He was tired from the drive and the strain of trying to humor Ms. Adams, and he wanted nothing more than to collapse for a while and go over his lecture. But, of course, he couldn't leave Stephanie sitting in the lobby, so he explained what had happened and invited her to come back to his room and wait there. "I'm not at all surprised," she said wearily, as if she had already decided in advance that the day was going to be a total loss. They walked down a long motel corridor covered with new-smelling, floral-patterned carpet; he unlocked the door and swung it open for her, then dragged in behind and set his bags down next to the bureau.

The room was quite large and airy with two queen-sized double beds and a sitting area beside the window with three comfortable chairs. It reminded him of a room in one of the convention hotels where one could conduct interviews or have drinks and pretend not to be in a hotel room. The curtains were closed. Stephanie slumped into one of the chairs and stared at him. "May I take your coat," he said.

"No," she said, a little petulantly, as if she thought he might insist.

"Still a little chilly, I guess," he said. "Shall I turn the heat up?"

"Whatever."

He studied the thermostat and rotated its plastic wheel, then peeked out the window.

"A beautiful view of the parking lot," he said, folding the curtain back into place. "Would you like something to eat or drink?"

"No."

"I'm going to order something."

"A rum and Coke, I guess."

He tried Mary Fowler's number again, with no success after twenty rings, then placed an order for two rum and Cokes and two bags of potato chips.

"I suppose I'll end up staying here for the night," she said.

"At the Holiday Inn?"

"Wasn't that part of the plan?"

"They were supposed to put you up at one of the dorms, as I said. But if you'd rather stay here, that's okay too. We'll get it figured out, don't worry."

"I'll bet."

"Why are you in such a bad mood? Do you mind talking about it?"

"I'm not really. This is the way I usually am—the real me."

"If you say so."

"You might as well know the truth."

"You just seemed a little down, that's all."

"Very perceptive, Dr. O'Reilly. You're a shrewd man."

He dialed Mary Fowler's number repeatedly and let it ring and ring, but no one answered. Then he had the idea of phoning the Journalism Department, where someone did answer, a secretary who, it turned out, had never heard of him and had no information about his lecture. This seemed strange and alarming to him. Had he gotten the date wrong? All the faculty members, she said, had already left for the day. Their offices were empty; their doors were locked. He had no choice but to keep phoning the Fowler number until he could reach someone.

After the better part of an hour of this, until well after the drinks and potato chips arrived and while Stephanie waited impatiently, someone answered, a man's voice. At first he thought he had dialed the wrong number, but the voice turned out to be that of Professor Fowler's husband, just returned from work. He informed O'Reilly that his wife regretted any inconvenience but that she had received a surprise offer for a job interview—in Alaska, of all places—and had had to leave town unexpectedly that afternoon—but that she had left preparations for his appearance in the hands of several of her students. He would no doubt be hearing from them shortly, the husband assured him. O'Reilly was relieved but a little uneasy with the arrangements, which seemed haphazard, everything thrown together at the last minute as Mary Fowler was hurriedly beating it out of town. The husband, clearly, was taking no responsibility for any of this and wanted nothing more than to hang up and go eat his TV dinner. He was barely polite. O'Reilly had no choice but to wait there with Stephanie, trying to make idle chitchat, until the students contacted him.

"You won't believe this," he said when he hung up. "The woman who invited me here has gone to Alaska!"

"You don't have to lie, you know."

"No kidding. I just talked to her husband. That's what he said."

Stephanie took a sip of her drink, then slid her finger slowly around the rim of the glass. "I know all about your reputation," she said. "But I haven't decided yet what I'm going to do about it."

O'Reilly thought it better not to respond to that one. She was tired and already a little drunk, it seemed, maybe even a little on the neurotic side. Peculiar, he thought, that he hadn't noticed any hint of it before. Of course, he hadn't known her for very long, and up until then their relationship had been quite formal. What did she mean, his "reputation"?

So far as he knew, he didn't have a "reputation," or rather, his reputation was a good one at the small private college in central Ohio where he had worked for the past fifteen years, teaching primarily journalism courses. He was on the verge of being promoted to full professor, and that didn't happen without a good reputation.

After the breast cancer had taken his wife, he passed through a period of bereavement and despondency when he was out of touch for a while with campus concerns, with faculty social life, and more distanced, too, from his students. He knew that. He found it more difficult now to make small talk, to focus on others' perceptions and needs. But he didn't believe it had damaged his reputation.

He was still essentially the same man, more sad-faced and moody beneath his drooping mustache, dragging himself around campus like an old arthritic hound; more apt to waste time zoning out in front of a ball game on TV with a beer on the armrest—just to clamp a lid on memory— but still idealistic in his own way, committed more than ever to his work, temperamentally somewhat shy and low-key actually, traits which were occasionally mistaken for aloofness, or, alternately, as timidity or weakness.

Students who tried to take advantage of this misapprehension by bullying O'Reilly soon learned they had misread the man. He was, in fact, disciplined and tenacious to the point of occasional stubbornness and inflexibility. But he was a fair-minded teacher. That hadn't changed. He was lucky enough to have been influenced by several exceptional teachers himself, and he had, in many ways, internalized their styles and attitudes and made them his own and built upon them. He was well liked by many of his students when they got to know him, and quite close to a few of them, but always in the role of a mentor and friend, nothing else. Of course, in a small community, there were always rumors concerning hanky-panky of various sorts. Maybe she had picked up on some ridiculous rumor.

It was his opinion that the "lecherous professor" of popular mythology, who traded grades for sexual favors, was pure myth, or at least, so rare as hardly to constitute a valid statistical probability. He resented the stereotype because it tended to discredit the profession. Students sometimes developed crushes, and gossiped about them, but these were, after all, typical of adolescence and not to be taken seriously. If they didn't fixate on one of their teachers, it was just as likely to be some rock star or professional athlete, someone safe and unattainable to fuel their fantasies until they moved on to a more mature relationship. Sometimes it was merely a sign of abstract admiration or even of engagement or excitement with the subject matter, which the student confused with love, in which case, seen from his point of view, the emotion could have a positive side that merely needed focusing. After twenty years of teaching, he imagined he had dealt with just about every shading that such attachments might take.

A loud knocking at the door caused Stephanie to start.

"Oh, hurray!" she said bitterly. "It must be them."

O'Reilly got up to answer it.

Three young men were standing out in the hall. When they found they had come to the right room, each of them shook hands with O'Reilly. The one wearing a crooked polyester tie seemed to be the spokesman. He was heavyset and had muscular shoulders and looked uncomfortable in the button-down shirt.

"Oh, sorry," he said as they filed in, "we didn't know you brought your wife." Stephanie stood up, looking awkward and embarrassed.

"No, no," O'Reilly said. "This is Stephanie Adams. She's a journalism student in our department who has come along to observe."

"Oh, sorry," the boy said again, in a tone that sounded, perhaps unintentionally, sarcastic. He winked at the others and moved toward Stephanie to shake hands, beaming an Ultrabrite smile at her that was off-center and dangerous.

"We're so glad you could come," Stephanie said, in a tone only slightly less aloof than one might have expected from a member of the royal family.

During his presentation, he noticed that Stephanie had forgotten to turn on the tape recorder. He didn't want to interrupt the flow to signal to her, but he was hoping to use the tape as a basis for starting an article (as he had emphasized to her), so he was greatly relieved when, about twenty minutes into his talk, she remembered and clicked on the machine. At least he would have the last half. Occasionally, Stephanie would scribble a note on her pad or she would raise the camera to her face, stare at him fixedly through the viewfinder, her lips screwed up in a sullen little scowl, and snap the shutter. She was going through the motions but she was certainly not enjoying herself; her misery was evident for anyone to see. She acted as if she found the work in some way demeaning. Though she was sitting up front near the boys who had served as their hosts, it had taken her about five seconds to size them up as rubes and creeps, and she had spoken scarcely a word to any of them.

Did beautiful women have the same problems as ordinary women? Perhaps they were more irritable because they scared away the men, made them feel inadequate. A girl this beautiful, you automatically assumed she was already spoken for. If you were a kid, you might not even try to get to know her for that reason. Or maybe it was the other way around. Beautiful women had to fend off passes so often that they grew cynical, assuming all men were "after" them in some sense and couldn't be trusted. Early on, they would develop all the signals that said "keep your distance" and "go away and leave me alone." *Was this Stephanie's problem?* he wondered.

The Brockton students had no information about arrangements for Stephanie to stay in the dorms—probably Mary Fowler hadn't gotten around to that—so, afterwards, O'Reilly asked Stephanie if she would have any problem coming back to the Holiday Inn with him. He was afraid she might be disappointed to miss the chance to be in the dorms and to meet other students, but after the way she treated the Brockton students, he doubted it.

"Why not?" she said, "it's just a bed," as if she still believed, for some reason, that these arrangements were part of some elaborate deception on his part, for some purpose he did not want to think about. He thought he had suffered just about enough of her snottiness for one day. When they got back to the Inn, he marched her up to the front desk and said, "Give this young lady a room," and he paid for it and told her he would meet her at the desk in five minutes with her luggage. On his way back down the long hall with her things, he saw her standing outside one of the doors and she motioned for him to deposit the bags inside, which he did, then paused momentarily at the door in order to make plans for leaving in the morning.

Stephanie said she was sorry but she had some bad news for him: she had forgotten to turn on the tape recorder until about halfway through his lecture.

He said he had noticed. "You didn't seem to be enjoying yourself much tonight," O'Reilly said.

"It's not exactly exhilarating work, is it?"

"It's *work,* if that's what you mean, and the hardest part is the rest of the assignment."

"Writing it up, you mean, or inviting you in for a nightcap?" Her eyes snapped at him as if to register some point that should now be understood between them, but he was afraid he had missed the point, whatever it was. He was tired. Was she inviting him in or telling him to buzz off? He was not at all sure he wanted to know. It was not a message, he felt, she needed to communicate. Why did she think she had to treat him like an eighteen-year-old? He certainly wasn't going in, he knew that much. He intended to excuse himself and go to bed.

"The writing," O'Reilly said.

"I doubt if I'll do much better at that, either."

"Why do you say that?"

"You don't know?"

"No."

"I was rejected by the Newspaper Fund."

"No, I didn't know. That's too bad."

"That recommendation of yours must have really done the trick, Dr. O'Reilly."

"It must have," he said, shaking his head, then realizing she wasn't kidding. Her eyes were welling up with tears. "You don't think that was the reason, do you? You don't think I would do that to someone, do you?"

"It wouldn't surprise me in the least," she said.

"Thanks a lot."

"No, I suppose it was a variety of factors," she said, dabbing angrily at her eyelids.

"It's a very competitive program. I'm sure there were a lot of good people who didn't make it," he said.

"I suppose."

"Maybe you could try again next year."

"Maybe you could write me another stunning recommendation."

"Well, I am sorry it didn't work out for you, Stephanie. Really, I am."

She broke into tears and turned to close the door but instead bumped awkwardly into his shoulder, holding on for a moment and muffling her sniffles into his coatsleeve.

"Better call it a night," he said, patting her arm in a paternal way, keeping her at a distance. "Things will look better in the morning. We can talk about it some more."

The winds blew ferociously all night long, and the weather report, in the morning, predicted a rapid drop in the temperature and a blockbuster snowstorm heading toward them, with gale warnings and severe conditions and travelers' advisories. O'Reilly rushed to get underway before the storm hit, but the snow was soon falling, and the trip back took them until late afternoon, a hard drive through the worst blizzard of the season. Stephanie was as uncommunicative as she had been the day before, and he was distracted by the bad weather, fighting the wind and the white-outs just to keep the car on the road. He thought about bringing up the subject of her rejected application but thought it might be better to let it rest. By the time O'Reilly pulled up in front of Stephanie's dormitory and let her out and watched her dash inside, it was a good ten inches deep and still blowing, and his wheels got stuck in the slush next to a drainage grate and dug in. He was mired there, foundering in the drifts, exhausted and embarrassed, alternately spinning his tires and hopping out to claw and kick at the snow, in full view of a thousand windows outside her dormitory, trying hopelessly to free himself, until finally three boys happened past, looking very much like the ones who had come to his rescue the day before. They lowered their shoulders and cried "heave-ho" and off he chugged, at long last, into the teeth of the storm, waving his thanks and watching them wave back.

As winter slowly ebbed, Stephanie appeared twice a week at his office for her Independent Study course. From his window he could see her coming down the walk between the ridges of snow, her blond curls tucked into the fur-trimmed hood of a melon-colored ski jacket. When she arrived, threw her coat across the rack, and sat down in the chair beside his desk, her cheeks glowed. Her disposition was never predictable—she was alternately sullen, buoyant, rude, or ingratiating—but during those weeks she did seem, gradually, to have forgiven him for whatever it was she imagined he had done to ruin her chances for the internship. She always looked as if she had just stepped fresh from the shower, then spent two hours putting on her face, taking special trouble with her mascara and eyeliner, her hair, her clothes.

Unfortunately, it began to be clear to O'Reilly that she did not spend the corresponding time and effort on her assignments for him. Her articles were often late, and they were neither polished nor very interesting or perceptive. She had started out by reading an article in *Cosmopolitan,* one of her favorite magazines, she said, and trying to imitate the chummy, personal style of the piece, but her article—on "Who Gets Ahead and Why"—was vague and vacuous and full of dubious conclusions in addition to taking an amazingly condescending and self-important tone. Then when she read articles in *The Atlantic, The New York Times Magazine,* and *Saturday Review,* at his suggestion, and tried to imitate their more intellectual or objective styles, she kept repeating the same patronizing, overly familiar tone of the first assignment.

When he tried to show her where she was getting off the track, she seemed not to get the point and to stubbornly resist his suggestions for revision, as if she knew better than he did what was necessary. She thought she knew what the young, hip generation of which she was a part wanted to read and how they wanted it to sound. She implied that he was stodgy and out-of-date and too concerned with style, with research and factual data. She used the incomplete tape recording as an excuse to avoid altogether writing the report of his talk at Brockton, especially since she had lost the notes. It became increasingly obvious to O'Reilly that she had no aptitude for the work, not even very much interest in it, and that she did not accept criticism well, even when offered in the most tactful and generous ways.

Toward the end of the semester, she informed him that she realized her enthusiasm for journalism had been premature, that what she wanted to be now, her "true destiny," she felt sure, was a high-level executive. She could see herself working for some major corporation, IBM or Chase Manhattan, she said, in some managerial role, though she knew that would be difficult since she was a woman and there were incredible sexist barriers out there to overcome. She had just read a wonderful book called *The Female Executive* and another one called *Winning through Intimidation,* and these had given her a whole new perspective on herself and the possibilities that lay ahead. She knew she had to take charge of her life now and be more assertive in general, and she knew that she had the potential to do just that.

O'Reilly listened carefully. He wasn't clear what her future in the business world might be, but he was relieved she had ruled out journalism because, so far as he could ascertain, she would have made a mediocre journalist at best. If his course had helped her find that out, he concluded that it had probably been worth the price of admission. A few weeks later, when it came time to assign grades for the semester, he went over her papers again, wavering between a C+ and a B-, and finally decided on a B-, preferring to err in the direction of generosity.

A few days later, during finals, Stephanie came storming into his office, and he knew by the peevish expression on her face even before she opened her mouth that she must have found out her grade, which he had posted on his door with the others. She slumped into the chair beside his desk and glared at him.

"I can't believe you had the nerve to give me a B- in that course after all the work I put in!"

Yes, he did, he said. It was no mistake. He told her he knew she had undoubtedly worked hard but that his evaluation also had to cover the quality of the work and her overall progress and to compare it with others who had taken the same course. It was his standard reply. He didn't feel she had worked very hard, in fact, but maybe she thought she had.

"So now you're telling me I'm stupid, I suppose."

"Not at all. . . ." He told her the grade was simply a measure of her performance in this particular instance, not a comment on her overall intelligence. "And, really, I don't know what you are so upset about. B- is a perfectly respectable grade."

"Not when I earned an A, it's not."

He told her that, unfortunately, he was the person who decided what she had earned; and in his opinion, she deserved a B-, and, in his opinion, that was a generous evaluation, in her case.

"In your opinion!"

"In my opinion."

"What would get you to change your opinion?—anything?"

"Not at this point, I'm afraid. The grade is already recorded."

"You're telling me there is absolutely nothing I can do to change that grade."

He told her he thought she would be far better off trying to understand why she had received the grade rather than trying to justify herself by blaming it on him.

"I think I know the reason all too well."

"Okay."

"Does that mean you won't change the grade?"

"I won't change the grade."

"If you weren't such a sexist snob, there wouldn't be any problem about this grade, did you know that?"

He told her he thought the "problem," such as it was, was with her performance, not with his evaluation of it, and until she acknowledged that possibility he said he didn't know how she could expect to improve her work in the future.

"I wouldn't want to improve according to your terms, believe me, Dr. O'Reilly. The *problem* is that I didn't smile enough and brown-nose you the way everyone else does."

"Unfortunately, I do not give grades for smiling, although some people persist in thinking that I do. If I did, I'm sure you would have received an A."

"Goddamn you! Sure, I would have. That or gone to bed with you in that Holiday Inn. That's what you wanted, isn't it?"

"Stephanie, you can keep bringing up irrelevant points all day long, and it's not going to change anything. I think you had better go home and cool off."

"That was my biggest mistake right there at the Holiday Inn, wasn't it, Dr. O'Reilly, and now you're making me pay for it."

"If you would like to bring your papers back in and sit down with me in a sensible frame of mind, Stephanie, we can go over them again and I will try to give you a detailed explanation of why you received a B-. As it is, I don't think we're getting anywhere." She stood up quickly and squinted at him with such unremitting hatred that he wouldn't have been surprised if she had spat in his face.

"I have no intention of bringing in my papers again and sitting around your stupid office being bored while you stare up my skirt."

"Either way, it's up to you."

"You bastard," she said under her breath and turned and marched out the door.

Well, it was too bad that she had gotten so upset. He regretted it, but he wasn't going to change the grade, and she seemed determined to get angry if he didn't, so what could he have done? It was a professional liability, this occasional confrontation over grades, and one part he disliked most about his job.

In Strickland's musty office, as the department head sat puffing on his pipe and staring out the window, O'Reilly read Stephanie's letter. Stephanie described how, in utter frustration, she had actually gone to see the Dean to complain about O'Reilly's unprofessional conduct. "I responded unfavorably to what I see as an entire semester of seduction," she said, "and was punished academically for it."

According to Stephanie, O'Reilly tried to get her drunk in a motel room on a trip to Brockton College. He tried to get her to spend the night in his motel room. He told her she couldn't have an A in his journalism course *unless* she slept with him. . . . *How could she lie so blatantly? What had he done to deserve this?* According to Stephanie, he was guilty of leaving his gradebook in plain sight on the corner of his desk, "like a threat."

Strickland was a fussy, gossipy, excitable little man with pointed, ratlike ears and the physical mannerisms of an elderly woman. He had postponed saying anything about it, he told O'Reilly, until he had had a chance to discuss it with other senior members of the department. They had never had a case quite like it before, he said, at least not since he had been chairperson, and certainly never involving a candidate for promotion to full professor. He affected great concern and an open mind, then asked to hear O'Reilly's "version" of what had happened. When O'Reilly told him, Strickland's face showed a barely repressed incredulity.

Strickland didn't like him, he knew that. Strickland had been one of the few senior members of the department, O'Reilly had heard on good authority, who had voted against O'Reilly's promotion. But to be enjoying O'Reilly's embarrassment as much as he obviously was seemed crude and uncivilized, not to mention ominous.

So far as O'Reilly could remember, he had never been impolite to Strickland, though he had had ample reason. He had never given Strickland any special reason to dislike him, though privately, he regarded the man as an inflated old windbag. His area of specialization was fairly far removed from Strickland's, so it might have been said that they had little in common professionally. But the same was true of many of his other colleagues without anything like the same uncomfortable sense of enmity.

Strickland, who had never published anything, was especially critical of O'Reilly's publications. Whenever O'Reilly published something, Strickland invariably saw it as "merely journalism" or as evidence of self-interest. Strickland was presumably dedicated only to the welfare of the institution as a whole, not to flaunting his own work. As a dedicated altruist, he had made campus politics his chief concern for thirty years, he knew everyone, and his opinions carried a great deal of influence. "So you think it's a case of someone going off half-cocked," Strickland was saying.

"I think it's a case of retribution for imagined injury," O'Reilly said, "which now borders on . . . slander."

"Thank you for your input," Strickland said. He stood up and ushered O'Reilly toward the door, after suggesting that O'Reilly put everything in writing for the Dean's benefit since O'Reilly would, of course, be seeing the Dean first thing on Monday morning. Strickland had already made the appointment.

O'Reilly had never been suicidal before that weekend, but shortly after his meeting with Strickland he began to comprehend the urge for suicide, for oblivion, in a new way. Saturday was a haze of writing, walking, and recriminations, of cup after cup of burning coffee and long-winded lectures to unwilling imaginary audiences. Then the better part of Sunday afternoon he spent alternately sitting in a small park near the local gorge and gazing at the river below from a dizzying height as he leaned against the guard rail on the suspension bridge and tried to think of reasons why he should not jump. The hum of the water and the flutter of heat waves above the weeds along the winding shoreline were hypnotic. He could so easily imagine the long swimming down through the air, the flapping descent like an awkward dive, the sudden, thrilling speed and emptiness, the senses lost in the whirl and the warm wind and the distant foam, and the absence, the release. Would he want to stop halfway down and change his mind? He thought not. If he stood there too long, he feared he would feel the desire to leap rising into his mouth like the metallic taste of lust. He got into his car and drove rapidly away.

The Dean greeted O'Reilly warmly and then sat down at his matched wood-grain desk to read O'Reilly's letter. An attractive vase containing fresh-cut flowers was positioned on one marble sill, and the lawns beyond the Dean's windows, which faced front campus, were suddenly dense with students changing classes. The Dean was such a brisk, dapper, well-balanced man, he made O'Reilly feel shaggy and tired. In the spotless, well-appointed office, with its plush carpet, with its bronze and lucite paperweight and ivory inlaid letter opener lying there ready for use, O'Reilly's hold on reality felt wafer thin, in danger of slipping away.

"Miss Stephanie Adams' letter—which I have just read for the first time—is a ludicrous fabrication based upon, but frequently departing from, an accurate account of her acquaintance with me," his letter began. *Was any of it believable?*

After reading O'Reilly's letter and asking a number of questions, especially about O'Reilly's intentions to sue the girl if she persisted in defaming him, the Dean took the position that O'Reilly had clearly been wronged and that he should be protected from further insult in every way possible. "A lawsuit, however, is not a good idea," the Dean warned. "Such cases are the devil to prove, and all you end up with is a lot of unfavorable publicity, both for you and for the institution. And, of course, the expense can be overwhelming." O'Reilly agreed.

The Dean wasn't at all certain that the information could be kept from the Professional Standards Committee, however, which was then in the process of considering O'Reilly's promotion, though, of course, O'Reilly's letter of defense (which was enormously persuasive, in the Dean's opinion) could also be included. He was certain that one isolated complaint of this kind was not a sufficient basis to bring O'Reilly up before the Committee on Termination for Cause.

Since Stephanie Adams had indicated to the Dean that several other young women who had worked for O'Reilly as assistants had complained privately to her that they had been harassed by O'Reilly, the Dean had instructed the associate dean in charge of on-campus employment to look into these allegations and to keep track of any other complaints that might be made in the future. The Dean was pleased to say that the associate Dean had turned up no evidence against O'Reilly whatsoever, only good reports, but he still felt it necessary to warn O'Reilly that any additional complaints would have to be taken very seriously.

When O'Reilly expressed his alarm at the spreading circle of administrators, faculty, and students who had had cause to learn about his predicament with all its potential for damage to him, the Dean assured O'Reilly that he had, of course, emphasized the need for confidentiality when he had spoken to the associate dean and to the chairman of the Professional Standards Committee, and, believing in the professionalism of his colleagues, the Dean was reasonably sure that O'Reilly had nothing to worry about in that respect, though, needless to say, it was a regrettable situation and put O'Reilly in a very difficult position; he realized that, no matter what others might do to try to help him and to clear his name.

The Dean advised patience and forbearance, on O'Reilly's part, and "waiting it out" and assured him of his continuing support. O'Reilly thanked him, shook the offered hand, and drifted out of the Dean's office and down the long hall with its gilt-framed paintings of dead benefactors and former presidents of the college, who seemed to be judging him with their stern, intense faces.

So far as O'Reilly could tell, everyone he passed in the hall or across campus, as he headed toward class, knew or thought they knew that O'Reilly was a lecher and a disgrace, and there was not one word he could utter, not a thing he could do, to change it. For years afterwards, O'Reilly carried this knowledge like another form of bereavement. At first, it was like a knot in the pit of his stomach, but eventually it was like an old wound he would sometimes aggravate purposely just to call forth the memory of the anguish and despair he was feeling now. Because however much it throbbed and festered as he lugged it around the campus or around the drab, anonymous streets of the city where he eventually settled to work as a reporter for a second-rate newspaper, at least it let him know he was still alive and reminded him vividly of the life he had left behind.

Bloomville

All our lives together, my father and I waited for the Cincinnati Reds to win the World Series, and they never did—except the year before I was born and the year after he died. Already, as a teenager, when I couldn't sleep from grieving over the errors and failed opportunities that had cost the Reds the game that day, I learned that you don't place your only chance for happiness on factors so utterly beyond your control.

During much of my childhood and adolescence, my father worked as a traveling salesman and he was often absent during the week, but he always came back to us. Perhaps that was the greatest impression he made upon me during those years, that no matter how far away he traveled, no matter what dangers he faced—obscene traffic, Japanese kamikazes during the war, planes veering out of control, vicious businessmen, muggers, murderers, the Mafia—he always came back to us, his face weary, his shoulders tightening under the weight of briefcases and luggage at the door. It began to seem almost magical when I considered the odds against him—his bellicose attitude behind the wheel of the Oldsmobile, his desire to pass everyone on the road, cursing in a cloud of Camel smoke, the sheer frequency of his trampings up and down the stairs of furious airliners—that he always beat the odds and returned. I must have worried that he wouldn't survive the dangers I imagined for him, but what I remember is my sense that his survival was somehow magical, that his bond with us was a kind of charm that would always bring him safely home.

Each day, when I visited my father at the cardiac-surgical unit of the Texas Medical Center, I used to pass Dr. Cooley's car in the doctors' lot on my way from the Tides Motel across the street. It was a customized Cadillac, black as an undertaker's limousine, and with a private nameplate

103

that read Denton Cooley, M.D. It made me think of the mountains of money Cooley must be raking in from desperate and dying people like my father.

In a book about Cooley I had bought at the airport on my way in and read from each night at the Tides, while my mother leafed through magazines and tried to watch TV, I learned that several other doctors would precede Cooley and perform the surgery for opening up the chest cavities. Then, at the crucial moment, Cooley would enter the operating theater, moving briskly from room to room, and on each table he would find a patient whose open heart was glistening and wobbling, and he would immediately seize the heart and do what had to be done. He was the medical equivalent of Roger Staubach—the operation truly started as soon as the ball was in his hands.

But it wasn't as if he was mass-producing open-heart operations for purely pecuniary reasons, I told myself. It was because there were so many seriously ill people who needed his care and because he was the best. A man of his skills and stature deserved to be well paid. I think I wanted to admire Dr. Cooley because I knew my father's life was in his hands.

In the late afternoon, I used to drive over to a track I had located on the campus of Baylor University and put in some laps. The day before the operation I got in a conversation there with one of the other runners, a pleasant-looking, bald-headed man—he had noticed my Duke T-shirt and wanted to know if I had done my medical work at Duke—and I said no, that I was a librarian, in fact, from upstate New York, and that I had only been an undergraduate at Duke and that I was in Houston because tomorrow my father was going to have a heart operation.

"Cooley?" he said, and I nodded. It turned out that he was an obstetrician who happened to have been Dr. Cooley's college roommate. At first, I thought he was putting me on. He said Cooley had been an incredible athlete as a young man, a gifted basketball player. I thought of Cooley's large, delicate hands, his spatulate fingertips with enormous moons, cradling the ball. The bald-headed obstetrician wanted to talk about Cooley's nobility and his success with women. He said my father was in good hands—none better. I decided he probably *had* been Denton Cooley's roommate, and although I am the world's least superstitious person, I wondered what it meant, if anything, that I had met him under such circumstances.

Neither my mother nor I slept well that night at the Tides. Early the next day, we ate a light breakfast and plodded across the parking lot past Cooley's Cadillac to the huge beige hospital building. There is a special room where the families of Cooley's patients await news from the staff on that morning's operations. Quickly, the room filled up with worried-looking people. We spent the morning crowded together like passengers in an airline departure zone who expect to hear the plane has crashed upon arrival—reading, looking at one another, and trying to block out the sounds the bored children were making.

Finally, in early afternoon, Dr. Cooley himself appeared and began talking to one of the families. A wave of energy and expectation washed across the room. Cooley said a few words, smiled in a controlled, non-committal way, and moved on to another group. It was evident that he intended to report personally on each patient. We could hear the music of his soft Texas accent as he moved from family to family but not what he was saying. He was a tall man, a commanding presence among us, still wearing the pale green surgical gown and the cap, like some sort of priestly or extraterrestrial visitor conducting a somber communion ceremony, and everyone in the room was extremely attentive.

The waiting was painful. Already, other families were filing out, the relieved rumble of their talking and occasional laughter echoing back down the hall. My mother and I were among the last to hear. Cooley placed his hand on my shoulder, and I was conscious of the nearly empty room surrounding us. "Your father didn't have an easy time of it, Mr. Townley," he said, "but he seems stable at present. He experienced arrhythmia and heart failure on the table while they were wheeling him into the operating room and several times during the operation as well, which made the operation rather difficult and long. The valve was severely damaged, only a flap really, and the heart very weak. We replaced the valve and performed a bypass operation in two locations, using veins from his legs, as we had described. I don't know how he made it to that room, but we'll hope for the best now."

"Thank you so much, Dr. Cooley," my mother said. Cooley hesitated a moment, eyes downcast toward the carpet as if searching for words to say something else. Already I began to feel an ominous sense that he was spending too much time with us, and the tone was pessimistic. Cooley nodded matter-of-factly and I could feel the pressure of his hand leave my back as he turned to go, and I regretted that we had so little time to discuss the situation. But he was obviously a tired man with other important work demanding his attention. I hugged my mother, and we walked out into the hall in a daze and on out into the blinding Texas sun.

We were permitted to visit my father in the recovery room for the first time that night. We kept our appointment in the same ward but in a different room with all the same people who waited with us so long earlier. Their now familiar faces were becoming part of the nightmare. We were given warnings and guidelines by the hospital staff. We were to be allowed into the recovery room a few at a time, only after we had been called by name, and for a very brief period of time. We were not to expect too much on this first visit—most of the patients were still unconscious or sedated. We were escorted down an immaculate white corridor and asked to wait. About twenty of us—names called by the nurse—stopped in a cluster outside the first door, blocks of colorful shirts and dresses pressing against the walls. The others walked farther down the long hall and disappeared around the corner.

The smell of ether and ammonia and something sweet and antiseptic was overpowering at the door of the recovery room. Each time the names were called and some of our number entered, this odor drifted out. Inside, we glimpsed a scene as bright and hectic as the control room for a space launch, walls of monitors, beds situated at odd angles, stainless steel apparatus, tubes bubbling, hospital personnel hustling about with an air of authority. When "Townley" was finally announced, a doctor, one of Cooley's associates, Dr. Mason, accompanied us. We moved to the edge of my father's bed and hesitated there, looking down at him.

"You should not expect too much at this stage," Dr. Mason said. "It will take him a while to stabilize. . . . If you have any questions, I'll do my best to answer them."

"Thank you, Doctor," my mother said.

My father's eyes were open but eerily distant and full of pain and amazement. His mouth was drawn downward in a frightening way around the breathing tube. He pulled feebly against the adhesive tape with which his hands were tied to the aluminum bedrails, a kind of reflex action, as if he still didn't understand why they were tied. He wanted to yank the tube out of his throat. His mouth and lips were covered with mucous but dried and chapped-looking, and the stitching from the thoracic opening, black against the stain of orange disinfectant on his chest, extended from neck to navel, an enormous criss-crossing track across his breastbone that made him resemble a kind of Frankenstein, kept alive by the wires and tubes and IVs. I half-expected and feared he would stop breathing at any instant, or that his heart would stop, or that his face would show that horrified expression of the stroke victim.

"We're so grateful for Dr. Cooley's efforts," my mother said, "and for those of everyone involved." Dr. Mason, who could see we wanted to be left alone, excused himself.

My father's body seemed violated, brutalized. Of course, his bodily integrity *had* been ravaged. But one could actually see and feel his sense of victimization. He had been wounded, maimed, as if in battle. Even though he was still struggling, I sensed he was capable of giving up in response merely to this sense of invasion, to the enormity of it. Anger rose in my throat and chest as I began to identify with his misunderstanding. I wanted to fight back at Cooley and Mason and the self-important, white-clad nurses. If it would help, I wanted to tell him, I would fight to defend him against them. I would die myself, defending him—imagining myself gunned down and bleeding on the tile floor. I would not hesitate for an instant to do whatever was necessary. But there was a reason for this operation—remember that—I wanted to say. We wanted to make you well.

Later, after I had taken my mother back to the motel, I drove to the Baylor track and ran lap after lap around the pitch-dark oval, the distant streetlamps weaving spools of light around my head, until my heart was pounding as furiously as his might have been on the operating table, and I imagined my strength, my fresh blood, somehow feeding into his heart and his blood, making him well again. Then I collapsed on the stiff bleachers and watched the shadows of the tackling dummies in the infield and the stars and UFOs wheeling in merciless profusion across the night sky.

I remembered that as a high-school sophomore in Ohio, my father, Dick Townley, who weighed in at 140 pounds in those days, had played first-string tackle at Portsmouth High School—if you know what that means—before Depression conditions forced him to quit school and eventually take up sales work. That section of south-central Ohio has some of the most brutal football of any region of the country. That was where Woody Hayes used to come looking for his linemen, to Masillon and Ironton and West Portsmouth. Even in the twenties, a 140-pound lineman must have been an anomaly. He would have had to be quick, strong, and willing to take incredible punishment.

When I returned to the Tides, my mother was propped up on her bed watching the late movie. Her cheeks were shiny and her eyes looked suspiciously red. She said it was just about the saddest movie she had seen since *Gone with the Wind.*

The dream I remembered was about my father. Several members of our family—Gram, and my mother's sisters and my father's brothers—were gathered in the living room of our house in Cincinnati, the one we lived in when I was in high school, which we no longer owned. The radio was on and the Reds' first baseman, Ted Kluzewski, had just cracked a homer into the right field bleachers. On the floor in the middle of the room was my father, stretched out flat on his back asleep and wearing a pair of fluorescent boxing trunks. Then his eyes opened and he tried to sit up, as if he wanted to talk to us, but my mother scolded him and told him to lie down and behave as a dead person was supposed to behave. But my father ignored her. He rolled over and sat up and started to tell the exciting story of his operation, a blow-by-blow account. He actually watched the cutting, he said, which felt like someone pressing a melting ice cube to your flesh, and, when they were ready to sew him up, he did his part for the surgical team by holding the sutures for them like a Spanish dancer— in his teeth.

Each time we waited outside the recovery room door, the wait was a long one. We were usually the last to be invited in. Two or three nurses, residents, or inhalation technicians were always hovering near my father's bed, and he was attached to a special respirator which required a full-time technician to monitor it. He was still unconscious. Things were not going well. Each time we waited at the door past the ordinary visiting period, I feared the worst and tried to prepare myself. One time when Dr. Mason appeared suddenly and slipped past us through the door, I was convinced that he would walk slowly out and take us aside and tell us in his confident, patient manner that my father had had a crisis and had died inside the intensive care unit.

Many of the other patients were conscious now and joking with relatives. Our fellow visitors were becoming quite familiar to us—we saw the same faces, the same concerned expressions, each time we appeared—and they were beginning to show in their looks and growing respect and deference to us that they too understood that our case was one of the critical, perhaps hopeless, ones. Then, one day, these same concerned visitors were absent. Some could be seen lining up around the corner at a different door, and they looked back at us from down the hall, relieved that they had been promoted to a new level. New concerned visitors joined my mother and me from operations performed that day.

Waiting each day at the same door with the same stab of anxiety etching its way into my heart, the smell of the intensive care unit, which drifted out each time anyone entered and was unlike any odor I ever remember, began to nauseate me, and I had to breathe deeply and walk away from the door to keep from getting sick with the waiting. Some new patient whose bed was across from my father was hallucinating and jabbering each time we visited. He was a large, heavy-set man who talked endlessly and in great detail about taking a barge to an immense island in the sky. At one point, the beeping on one of my father's monitors stopped for several seconds, and the man was babbling about the beautiful blue barge, and no one seemed to be paying attention. I seized one of the nurses by the arm and pulled her toward the monitor, but it started beeping again and the nurse checked it and said, "No problem," and I told her I was sorry but I was afraid something was happening. "No big deal," she said. "Everything looks fine."

Then one day, after we had waited for about twenty minutes, a nurse came out and said she was sorry but Mr. Townley was no longer there. "No longer here!" I said, thinking he must have died in our absence. We were instructed to wait outside the door down the hall. Eventually Dr. Mason appeared. "He's finally out of the woods," Dr. Mason told us. Not only that, but when we approached his bed in the new quarters, we saw that the tube was out of his throat and his eyes were clearer. He was still weak, of course, but he recognized us and wanted us to sit on the bed. I grasped his hand and my mother took his other hand, and I said, "We're awfully glad to see you're feeling better."

"We knew you would be," my mother said, kissing him carefully on the cheek. "We never doubted it for a second."

He made a motion indicating that he wasn't able to talk but that my mother should hand him a pad and pencil that were lying on the bedside table. When she did, he held them and scribbled something and handed it to me, but the message was too illegible to be read.

"Okay," I said, "but you'll have to improve your penmanship." He started to smile but indicated that his lips hurt too much. A shrug was about all he could manage.

"It's all right," I said. "You'll be talking soon enough."

Later that week when I returned to see him, he noticed I was wearing a suit and wrote, "How come you are all dressed up?" and I had to tell him that I was here today to say goodbye, that I had to fly back home to see Annie and the kids in a few hours.

"But you're in good hands," I said. "You're going to be all right."

"I'm too tough to kill," he wrote. "Ask the U.S. Marine Corps and they'll tell you that, pal."

"I don't have to ask them," I said.

"My father was a traveling salesman and my mother was a farmer's daughter," I said, "but their marriage was no joke—not to me at least . . . and certainly not to you."

I pulled off to the side of the road and let the station wagon idle. Across the fields and the marsh, the familiar silver-roofed barns of my Grandmother Spalding's farm reflected the afternoon sunlight as if illuminated by some celestial beacon. I turned around to look at the kids in the backseat. I wanted them to remember this.

"When my father was selling vacuum cleaners door to door in 1938," I said, "if he hadn't driven down *this* road, you wouldn't be here today, and neither would I." The side-road I was talking about was paved but narrow and humped in the middle, a simple country road like many others in the area. The odds against his turning down that particular road forty years before seemed staggering.

"Let's go," my daughter said. "I really do have to pee, Papa."

"She was born having to pee," my wife said.

"Where are the cows?" my son said.

We were in north-central Ohio, just outside Bloomville in Seneca County, on our way to Cincinnati to visit my father, who had been very ill again, and my mother, who was exhausted by then, taking care of him. I wanted the children to know about his life because I was afraid he was dying.

My father, Dick Townley, had arrived outside Bloomville that day in 1938 from the river town of Portsmouth in southern Ohio. While he was trying to sell my grandmother an Airway vacuum cleaner, he saw my mother's picture in a gilt frame on top of the piano and said: "Who is that woman?" When my grandmother informed him that that woman was, in fact, not a woman at all but only her eldest daughter, who was not yet twenty years old, he said he thought her daughter had the loveliest eyes he had ever seen on a human face, including any movie star she would care to name. He went on to say that she might not realize it yet but that her daughter was indeed a woman and a very beautiful woman, and now that he looked more closely, he could detect a great deal of family resemblance between the two of them. Half an hour later, my grandmother bought the vacuum cleaner.

I should add that my father had a knack for selling vacuum cleaners, for selling anything. Selling vacuum cleaners, he had navigated the Depression years, and by 1935, at the age of twenty-seven, he was a branch manager, in which role he organized and directed the sales efforts of 118 men. He wore expensive suits and a rakish reddish mustache and drove a succession of sporty automobiles that were never more than a year old. My mother's father got one look at him and wanted to chase him away with his ten-gauge shotgun. In 1938, the year he eloped with my mother, my father's branch of Airway vacuum cleaners sold more sweepers in Ohio, Kentucky, and West Virginia than any other regional division in the country and were declared "International Champions."

He was a restless, good-natured, ambitious man who could charm the socks off total strangers but could not explain his talent for selling. "At some point in my salespitch, there is a critical moment. When I sense it, I hand them a pen and say, 'Sign on this line,' or 'You can't afford not to,' and they look me in the eye and take the pen and I point to the line and, even though they might not want to do it, they sign their names. It's an amazing thing—a gift—almost like hypnosis."

He was of Irish and English descent—he had the lightest blue eyes and a straight, well-defined, narrow-bridged nose—but his temperament was more characteristically Irish: affable, pugnacious, talkative, generous, argumentative, spontaneous, and proud. He was the second youngest son in a family of five boys and four girls, and his mother had been the youngest of twenty-five children. I suppose if her father, my great-grandfather, had been a reasonable and temperate man and had stopped at twenty-four children, my father would never have been born and I would not be here to tell about it.

Whenever my father took over a project or a business, he expected to turn it around overnight, to show measurable results almost immediately, to push it out of the red ink into the black. He built his entire career around such performances.

When the manufacture of electrical appliances was frozen during the war years, he moved his young family to Cincinnati and found a job selling radio time for WSAI. Maybe he wanted to prove that a man who could sell machines—hard goods designed for the removal of dirt—could also sell air. His sales total in the first year was equal to the output of the three other salesmen combined. He started to learn the radio business.

In 1944 he enlisted in the United States Marine Corps and was sent to officer's training school at Quantico, Virginia. One of my earliest memories is watching a long parade, my nose pressed against an iron fence, my mother holding me up high, while row after row of red, white, and navy-blue Marines file past. Somewhere out there, limber and tough, is my father; and we are straining our eyes to pick him out.

He was sent into the Pacific as an Air Support Control officer and was wounded on Okinawa by flying shrapnel and received 188 shots of penicillin and the Purple Heart. He was a captain. The day he came home in his uniform he walked right past me, sitting on my tricycle in someone's frontyard, without knowing who I was, but I didn't mind. He didn't like to talk about the war, and sometimes he would wake up in the night screaming. One night almost two years after the war was over, he leaped out of bed during some nightmare about the war and broke his toe on the chest of drawers.

He went back into radio, selling air time, then later, as an account executive, hitting the road again, selling syndicated radio programs to stations throughout Ohio and Kentucky.

In the late forties, he landed a job in Pittsburgh, Pennsylvania, as general manager of one of the big, downtown, city radio stations; and we moved from a modest buff-brick with a bare, fenced-in backyard in a subdivision to an English-Tudor-style mansion on a hill in Fox Chapel, Pennsylvania, a glitsy, wooded suburb. That year Mr. Haan, who lived down the block and who owned a furniture store and was my friend Jimmy's father, brought home the first TV set anyone I knew had ever seen. It had a seven-inch porthole screen, and all the kids in the neighborhood hunched in front of it for hours every day until Jimmy's mother chased us out of the house. Mr. Haan said he thought it was just a gimmick, a passing fancy, but my father maintained that it was the wave of the future and that the world would never be the same.

The end of our lives in Pittsburgh was brought on by a terrible automobile accident my father suffered in his brand new robin's-egg-blue Buick Roadmaster convertible, which he totaled on a rainy night by colliding with a steel and cement abutment. Both he and his secretary, who was a passenger in the car, were in critical condition for days but both survived. He crushed the bridge of his nose on the steering wheel and had to have his nose reconstructed by plastic surgery, but except for the scars it didn't look any different.

After that, my father took us back to Cincinnati, where he founded Townley Television, Inc., which, within two years' time, became the largest retail outlet for TV sets in Greater Cincinnati.

In 1951, when he was forty-three, my father sold Townley Television, Inc., and our new house and our boxseat at Crosley Field, packed up all our furniture, and we moved from Cincinnati to my mother's girlhood home in Bloomville, Ohio, a town of 750 people, to take over the farm for my Grandmother Spalding, who, since the death of my grandfather ten years before, had been victimized by a series of bad tenant farmers who were always "robbing her blind." Never mind that my father was not and never had been a farmer. The silver-roofed barns of Bloomville had always held a special fascination for him. He considered it a place of destiny. He had discovered my mother there, after all, and was under the impression that as he was the only male relative with any interest in or capacity for the pastoral life, the farm would eventually be at least partly his to inherit. He felt he had accomplished all he could as a merchandizer of TV sets. Now he could still be his "own boss" but would have the freedom to set his own schedule, get away from the heavy, tedious demands of running his own business, and breathe fresh air every day like a normal healthy human being, a kind of country gentleman. He poured his now substantial fortune into buying farm equipment, seed, fertilizer, and livestock.

We bought three huge International Harvester tractors, plows, rakes, mowing machines, a grain drill, a combine, a hay baler, a new stainless steel freezer for the dairy barn, twenty-nine head of dairy cattle that had to be milked at dawn and dinnertime every day of the year, a flock of over a hundred sheep, a barnyard full of brood sows, a chicken house full of laying hens; and there were over two hundred acres of tillable land that had to be plowed, grated, fertilized, planted, cultivated, and harvested. My father commuted to Ohio State two days a week to study agriculture under provisions of the GI Bill of Rights.

Almost from the first day he was embroiled in rabid arguments with my grandmother about how things ought to be done. She must have felt threatened by the sheer extravagance of his commitment and his obvious lack of experience. My grandmother was accustomed to ordering the tenant farmers around and to expressing her most paranoid fears about how they might be cheating her, accusing them of such behavior without a shred of evidence just in case they might be considering trying anything—in the mistaken idea that this would somehow prevent it. She had seen how things ought to be done on a farm for the last sixty years through direct observation, and she saw no reason why they ought to be done any differently now. Suddenly this new man, her son-in-law whom she had known previously as a vacuum-cleaner salesman, was marching up and down the land as if he owned the place, cruising by the front picture window in a great hurry on a brand-new twelve-thousand-dollar Farmall, trying to grow oats using some cockeyed formula for fertilizer he had read about in a book, planting all the crops in the wrong fields, and endangering the soil by stuffing it with nitrogen it didn't need.

My father was a man accustomed to giving orders, not taking them, and certainly not taking orders from a woman who was impolite, even if she was his mother-in-law, *especially* if she was his mother-in-law. Here he had changed his whole life, sold a prosperous business, moved his family, invested his life savings, and was, visibly and literally, knocking himself out, probably working himself into an early grave, giving every ounce of his strength to help her, and did she show even the slightest particle of gratitude? No, she didn't. Not only that, she openly implied that he didn't know what he was doing, didn't know what he was talking about, and that he might actually have set out to deceive her, that he might have some secret plan for taking over the farm and sending her to the poor house; and, short of that, even if he hadn't intended it, they were all going to end up in the poor house anyway because the farm was going downhill so fast at the rate they were going that they would both be bankrupt within the year.

In the beginning, I could barely lift a full pail of water, but my chores required the carrying of pail after pail. Within months, I could carry two two-and-a-half gallon pails of dry corn from the corncrib to the barnyard for the hogs or two full pails of water to the chicken coop or anywhere you wanted to take them, and I began to acquire respectable muscles in my arms for the first time in my life. In the course of a year I went from a skinny strike-out artist, the last kid picked for softball at the playground at recess, to one of the demon home-run hitters in the fifth grade.

Over that same year my father lost 40 pounds and pushed himself so hard physically that he developed tendonitis in both arms. He weighed 138 pounds, less than in high school, and his elbows hurt so severely that he couldn't pick up a cup of coffee without spilling it. My Uncle Doc came for a visit and advised my father that he would be dead inside another year if he didn't quit and find a more satisfying occupation. In the meantime, my father's farming methods had produced greater bushels-per-acre yields of corn, wheat, oats, and soya beans than had ever before been measured at the Bloomville mill. Our cows had higher and higher butterfat content in their milk, which brought in record receipts, and half-a-barnful of new calves. On the other hand, one of our sows gave birth to *nineteen* piglets but was so heavy and awkward she suffocated or bit and killed all but two of them. Chicken thieves broke into the henhouse, and several baby lambs wandered too close to the marsh and got entangled in the mud and undergrowth and eventually drowned or died of exposure.

One day, the brake slipped as my father was preparing to back into the low barn opening where he usually parked the tractor. Suddenly, the tractor started rolling backward and pinned his shoulders against the barn wall just above the framing. The angle of the small incline was just enough to keep the weight of the tractor locked against him and the steering wheel mashed tightly against his chest and under his chin in such a way as to make it impossible to reach the brake with either leg. He was barely able to get his toe on the clutch pedal in order to disengage the gears before he was crushed, but his purchase was so tenuous that he was reluctant to move for fear his toe would slip and the tractor would kick back into reverse. It was exactly the sort of freakish farm accident that one was always reading about in the local paper, just a matter of not ducking his head in time in order to clear the overhang. Pressed this way against the barn, unable to reach the gearshift or to dislodge himself, and feeling like the biggest horse's ass who ever tried to learn how to be a farmer, he called out for my mother and me. He shouted our names over and over again, as loudly as he could until he grew hoarse; but no one came to help. She was out of earshot, especially with the roar of the tractor drowning out his cries, and I was in school. Finally, after two hours of desperation, during which time my father had imagined the irony of his likely decapitation by means of his own tractor and his own carelessness so often that he was seething, and by which time his left leg was so stiff and numb that it had begun to shake precariously on the clutch pedal, the Farmall ran out of gas and he was able to release the clutch and, after some hard squirming, work himself free and stumble toward the house to tell the tale of his harrowing escape.

Ultimately, my father realized that Gram would never accept him there, no matter how well he performed, and that the struggle would always be a bitter one. He reasoned that if he went back into radio then, there would still be some openings. If he waited too much longer, he would have been out of circulation too long and no longer "a marketable commodity." At the end of a year and a half, we had an all-day sale and auctioned off every sheep, pig, and cow—each of which I knew by name and considered a close personal friend—every piece of farm equipment my grandmother didn't want to keep—all at a stupendous loss.

Somehow or other he had managed to secure a job as general manager of a prestigious station in Albany, New York, the state capital. After the tragedy of the sale, my father went almost instantly from frayed cotton flannel and down-at-the-heel clodhoppers, green with manure, to two-martini lunches, silk suits, and thirty-dollar neckties. Albany was the pinnacle of his career in radio. His offices and the studio were in the posh Ten Eych Hotel in the middle of downtown Albany and were owned by the Stines, who also owned ten other hotels, including the Ronnie Plaza in Miami Beach, and over one hundred movie theaters and were supposed to be worth around two hundred million dollars but were "impossible to deal with."

That year I was a bookish, bespectacled sixth grader who had a mysterious alternate life as a radio celebrity. For a month before Christmas, every day after school, I would report to the studio and tape a program with Santa Claus (who was impersonated by the program director). I was one of Santa Claus's main elves, named Bondy—the program was sponsored by Bond Bread—and I would read letters-to-Santa and tell stories about what Rudolph had done that day and give weather reports on the generally blustery conditions at the North Pole.

I would make personal appearances with Santa Claus at area schools and Cub Scout meetings, wearing a white apron and a baker's cap and pretending to be a more-or-less supernatural being, which was often the way I was treated. I hung around with other radio personalities at the station but especially our sports director, who during the summer months had another job—as first baseman for the Philadelphia Phillies—and because of his friendship, I once met and actually shook hands with Robin Roberts, who at that time was a young man and the greatest pitcher in baseball, even if he wasn't a Cincinnati Red. I also have a dim memory of being escorted with great fanfare by my father into a ballroom-size office at the Ten Eyck and shaking hands with Meyer Stine, whom I expected to look like a cross between Al Capone and a fire-breathing dragon but who, in fact, resembled no one so much as one of my kindly uncles. He held a gigantic cigar and smiled sweetly at me while he pumped my hand and seemed genuinely delighted to meet one of his more famous employees, a person—little did he suspect—who had, only the year before, been slopping the pigs, petting the cows, and conferring privately with a flock of chickens in Bloomville, Ohio.

But my father complained that the Stines were "eating him alive," always "on his back," no matter how well he did. Fairly soon, he began to feel that the job was too high-pressure, that there was too much tension. Now he could see why they had driven away every manager they had ever had. They were underhanded, devious, and had unsavory business connections that scared him to death. No decent man would want to work for them. If he didn't find something better, he was going to have an ulcer or a heart attack and that would be the end of it. His first year there, sales increased 250 percent.

We returned to Cincinnati, where he was spot-sales manager for a company syndicating TV programs. His territory was the eastern half of the United States. He paid visits to presidents of companies, whipped out his 16mm projector, and showed them installments of "Lassie," or "The Cisco Kid," or "The Millionaire," which were still new and exciting for the time, and tried to convince them to spend hundreds of thousands of dollars to sponsor the programs on national or regional television. Now he was using machines to sell air. He was on the road for weeks at a time. When I made the high-school basketball team, I remember telling him about it by a long distance call to some lonely motel room in West Virginia.

Before he started Townley Realty, he left Cincinnati and went back into radio one last time. I was in college by then in North Carolina. He and my mother moved to Florida, and he managed a problematic station in

Delray Beach, Florida. After two years under his guidance, the owners sold the station for seven times what they had paid for it three years before, and he was fifty-six years old with a heart condition and out of work and money again and very discouraged—too old for anyone to want to hire him for anything ever again, he said.

Within a year after they returned to Cincinnati and he started Townley Realty, he was driving a green Eldorado and opening up new branches all over the city. Every Sunday in the *Enquirer,* the smart little Townley Realty insignia were emblazoned all over the real estate pages. "I wish I had started in this business thirty years ago," he said. "If I had, right now I'd be a millionaire several times over and I could retire and play golf and spend some time at the ball park." He went from selling single family units, to apartment buildings, to skyscrapers. That was before inflation and interest rates went out of sight and knocked the bottom out of the real estate market and he was a sick, tired old man and the business was overextended and he lost his shirt.

When the valve Cooley had placed in my father's heart failed, my father could not afford another operation except under the auspices of the Veterans' Administration. (He had persuaded the VA that his heart condition was related to his Marine Corps service in the Pacific.) They flew him to Alabama on a military plane, and he went through the whole terrible ordeal of open-heart surgery a second time.

From various clues I had picked up over the phone following that operation, I had the idea that his convalescence was not going smoothly. We spent two days driving across country to my parents' new, more modest, house in a Cincinnati suburb, the kids getting wilder and wilder in the backseat, then falling asleep early, lulled finally by the monotony—neon and the lights of passing trucks playing over their placid, trusting faces.

When we arrived in Cincinnati I was still groggy from the car, a rhythmic drumming in my ears, a slight sense of disorientation and claustrophobia. We searched for the place my parents had bought since my father's operation. It turned out to be a small brick house in a subdivision of nearly identical brick houses. We said our hellos—hello with a hug to my mother at the door, her face gaunt and shocking with its expression of grim resolution—as the children slipped past me to pet the yapping dog, and Annie followed me in with her polite, reserved greeting.

"Look who's here!" my mother crooned and led me to my father's chair. I thought she was about to introduce me to a neighbor. That is, for an instant, I did not recognize the strange man sitting there, who was obviously an invalid. He bore a surprising resemblance to my father but was clearly some other person. My brain seemed to misfire and I wondered if they had planned this meeting as some sort of inept practical joke. I was on the verge of laughter or anger at the thought. But there was such a terrible sadness and dignity about him that I realized I was mistaken. His eyes were my father's eyes but larger and unfamiliar. His cheeks had a peculiar sunken, taut quality I had never seen before, causing his face to seem thinner and more delicate, as if two giant hands had squeezed his cheekbones together. I had seen him tired before, but I realized I had never seen him in a condition when all the energy and animal vitality were completely absent from his body. It made me want to flee, to jump back in the car and try another house.

I made an effort to conceal the bewilderment and shock I knew must have registered on my face, but in addition to the uncharacteristic fluttering of elation in the eyes of the man in the chair, I detected something unmistakable then, some hardening of the mouth, an expression of disappointment—as if my father had hoped we wouldn't notice any change, and sizing up our embarrassed hesitation and forced cheerfulness, immediately resigned himself to it, as if to say: "It's that bad, is it? Well, all right, it's that bad then." It *was* my father; it was indeed my father, this shrunken figure with the peculiar face who seemed to parody the man I remembered from the first thirty years of my life, whose mannerisms I had made my own.

"Hello, pal," he said and held up his hand.

"How are you feeling?" I said, taking his hand and shaking it.

"About as miserable as a person could be and still be alive," he said.

"Where did you get that mustache?" I said.

He smiled. "It reminds me of the war," he said.

Except in photographs as a young man during his vacuum-cleaner days, I had never seen my father in a mustache. He had been of that generation of American men who believed—for most of his life—in the moral superiority of the clean-cut masculine look. Once when I had grown a beard in college, in fact, he had been surprisingly insulting about it. Now, what in the world was my father doing with this ridiculous mustache on his face?

"It gives me something to do," he said. "You wouldn't believe how boring it can get around here when you can't even walk around the block."

"How is he behaving?" I said to my mother.

"You know how he is," she said. "He watches the Reds game every night on TV, and if they lose, he frets about it half the night."

"That sounds like him," I said.

She wanted to show us the house, so we allowed her to lead us nervously from room to room. "It's not as large as *your* house, Annie, but it's about right for us. It's a cozy little house."

"It's quite attractive, quite nice," Annie was saying. She was trying to be polite. The two primary women in my life, my wife and my mother, had never had an easy time talking to one another.

These visits were often quite trying, in fact, which was one reason we avoided making them for as long as we could. Sad but true, I thought. Wasn't it the same everywhere these days: families cut off from their children, grown children living thousands of miles away, inaccessible, gradually becoming strangers to those who had raised them, rearing children of their own who could scarcely recognize their grandparents? It was a sign of something ominous, a breakdown in the machinery of American civilization. But what could be done about it? If this visit went well, maybe we could try harder to get together more often.

We returned to the living room.

My father said: "You know, pal, one of the doctors at the hospital came into my room just before we left, and he was looking me over and he said, 'Well, you sure have got good teeth for a man your age.' What do you think of that! I said, 'You may not believe this, but I used to be a helluva good man.'"

"You still are," my mother said from the other room, "if you could just get yourself healthy again."

"I'm not myself at all, pal. Gram called, and I cried on the telephone. You know me—I don't cry. I just haven't been myself lately."

My mother piped up to say that she thought he must be on the road to recovery because of the way he yelled at one of the nurses the day they came home. "The nurse only came into the room to tell me that visiting hours were over and the curtains were to be kept open. But Dad didn't care for the tone of her voice. 'Who do you think you're talking to?' he said. 'I'm Dick Townley, and this woman is my wife. We've been married for thirty-seven years, and I won't have you talking to her that way! No one talks to my wife like that, and you'd better not forget it!' He insisted on seeing the director of the hospital to demand an apology."

"That sounds like him," I said.

"That poor nurse," my mother said. "I was so embarrassed I didn't know what to do."

"She deserved every bit of it," my father said. "The next time maybe she'll try to show a grain of compassion for her patients. It's not easy when you're as sick as I am being at the mercy of those people. You have to show them who they're dealing with."

• • •

The next morning I learned that my father wasn't supposed to be home at all. "Are you kidding?" I said to my mother, who was cleaning up the breakfast dishes.

"Well, they wanted him to stay a few days longer, but he was bound and determined to come home. He said he wanted to watch the Reds game on his own television set and sleep in his own bed."

"And you agreed to that?" I said.

"It was the best decision I ever made in my life," my father said from his chair. "They were getting rich at my expense. That place was driving me crazy, pal. . . . To keep me there, one doctor even told Mom that I might have been experiencing some hallucinations. Imagine that."

"You weren't, were you?"

"They even had *me* wondering. All I can say is if they weren't hallucinations, there were some terrible things going on down there! I won't even bother to go into it—you wouldn't believe it. But I'll tell you, I feared for my life in that place."

"What do you mean?"

"The doctor said I couldn't go home—I wasn't physically able. My condition didn't allow it. I said it was *my life,* by God, and I know what I have to do and what I have a right to do. We had to sign papers saying we wouldn't hold them responsible for what might happen."

"That doesn't sound very sensible to me."

"I told the doctor: which would be better? To stay there and take a chance of someone putting a knife in my back or to come home where I could at least be comfortable. I'm telling you, I feared for my life in that place! It certainly is a relief to be home—so much quieter."

"Are you sure you're all right here, though? What if you need emergency treatment?"

"They had these reed-like things—respirators—they were all sucking on. There were four men in my room, and every one of them was sucking on one of these reeds."

"Oh, not all of them," my mother called from the kitchen.

"Yes, *all* of them! Yes they were. I *saw* them! They had fantastic equipment—I can't deny that. They had one of these respirators every twenty feet or so all up and down the halls—I bet they cost five hundred dollars apiece. Pretty nurses all decked out in blue uniforms would wheel the machines from room to room and they would say: 'Wouldn't you like to suck a little more on this reed now?' and 'Oh, that's not enough, have some more,' and 'Oh, come on, you can suck harder than that.' Finally, I asked one of the men there if those reeds weren't habit-forming, and he said, 'Yes, sir, Mr. Townley, they definitely are.' What do you think of that? My God, they had everybody in the hospital sucking on those things. . . . And all I can say is if we're going to depend on these men for the defense of our country, it's going to be one hell of an army. You never saw anything like it!"

Early in the afternoon, my father said he wanted to talk to me in private out in the backyard on the patio. We walked out together and sat down at a redwood table under a large gaily-colored canvas umbrella. He wanted to talk about what should be done after he died. I told him he wasn't going to die any time soon, so there was no need to worry about it. He said he had about ten thousand dollars in AT&T stock and a little money tied up in the house, but he was worried about what would happen to my mother when he wasn't here to take care of her any longer. I said he didn't have to worry about that as long as I was around. He said she was helpless as a baby and he was afraid her sisters would take advantage of her after Gram died. I said I wouldn't let that happen. He said he thought he'd made a terrible mistake spending so much money on his operations since it obviously hadn't done any good and maybe even speeded up his decline. He said he wanted me to remember that the farm in Bloomville was by far the most significant asset still in the family and that a third of it should eventually belong to me, but that I might have to fight for it. I said I would.

"There was a young man about your age in the hospital with me," he said, "and he was suffering from a coronary problem similar to mine, and they gave him a series of tests and decided he needed to have open-heart surgery. The doctors told him he had maybe two years to live unless he had the work done. He was an awfully nice fellow, thirty-four years old with several small children, and his wife was pregnant." He bent his head and pursed his lips and took a sip from his coffee cup.

"Yeah."

"Well, he was having a hard time deciding what to do, so the doctors asked me if I would talk to him and give him a little encouragement and I said I would. I told him I was a lot older than he was and I had been through it twice. I said it was tough but I thought he ought to be a man and go through with it. If the doctors were right, I said—and they knew a whole helluva lot more about it than he or I did—he could get his health back and live long enough to see his children grow up and otherwise he probably wouldn't. He said he had a bad feeling about it, that he thought maybe he should just quit smoking and change his diet and take care of himself and maybe his condition would clear up—since he was still so young. I said I was sure the doctors had already considered that or they wouldn't be advising him to have the operation. I said here he was in the hospital and the doctors were all ready to go as soon as he said the word—why didn't he go ahead and have it done and get it over with. Anyway, we went back and forth on this for a couple of hours, and I did my best to talk him into it and he finally agreed to it.

"Well, on the night before his scheduled surgery he got cold feet and decided he wanted to go home. So they wondered if I would talk to him again. He came down to my room, and he was in a terrible state. He was afraid he wouldn't live to see his new baby born. I said seeing him wasn't that important anyway. What was important was helping him to grow up and the only way that was going to happen was if he went through with the surgery. He said he just thought he needed some more time to think it over and make plans in case it didn't work out. I said I thought he was being needlessly pessimistic. I said here the doctors were all set to perform the operation the next morning and if he backed out now they might not be as willing the next time. I said he should be glad that he was able to live in a place where this kind of care was readily available, but he shouldn't take it for granted. Sometimes it wasn't easy to find a vacancy for this sort of major operation, especially for someone who had once had the opportunity and had turned it down. That could get expensive for the hospital. Sick people were lining up all over the country for these things, and so on. So, anyway, we went over everything about ten times, and I talked him into it all over again." He took another sip of his coffee.

"So what happened?" I said.

"He went into surgery the next morning, and he never made it off the operating table. He died."

"How did you find out about it?"

"They told me about it a couple of days later. They didn't want to mention it to me, but finally they did. I felt awfully bad about it, let me tell you. I still feel bad about it—just terrible."

"I can see why."

"And now those poor little children are without a father for the rest of their lives. Maybe I should have kept my big mouth shut."

"You thought it was the right thing to do. You were just trying to help. You can't hold yourself responsible."

"I know it. But that doesn't bring him back, does it. The fact of the matter is if I hadn't butted in he would be alive this minute. Maybe his gut feeling was right all along."

"Well, it's a horrible thing to have happen, but I think you ought to put it behind you. You have your own health to worry about."

"What health?"

The flies were bothersome and, without warning me, he picked up a can of Raid that was sitting on the windowsill and started shooting it around our heads. I ducked away but he kept spraying. I said not to aim it so close to our faces—it was poisonous. He suddenly got a frustrated look on his face and dropped his arms and then wound up and threw the can of Raid over the hedge out into the middle of the backyard and went inside, slamming the door. He really wasn't himself. I got up and followed him wearily into the kitchen. My father had gone to his bedroom. I was sorry our conversation had so quickly gone wrong—he was obviously in a delicate emotional state—but I thought maybe I should let him collect himself before I went in to see him.

Annie was just out of the shower and was sitting on the couch reading a magazine.

"Have you seen the kids?" she said.

"No," I said, "I've been out back." I sat down and picked up the paper.

She looked in our room and they weren't there. She came back and stood in the middle of the living room and stared at me while I was trying to read the paper.

"Where could they have gone?" she said.

"I don't know. Maybe my mother took them to the store with her."

"She wouldn't take them without telling us, would she?"

"I don't know. I don't think so. Didn't she say anything?"

"Not to me."

She went out the front door and walked around the house, searching for the children and calling their names. A few minutes later she came back in the same door.

"They're gone," she said. "How can you sit there so calmly?"

I got up and walked through the utility room and checked in the garage and walked on outside through the open garage door and around the station wagon, peering through the closed windows at the floor, littered with wrappers and tissues and small toys. I walked out to the curb and stared as far as I could see up and down the street, which suddenly seemed unnaturally quiet and deserted. When I went back inside, Annie was saying: "All right, if you kids are hiding somewhere in here, this game is over. It's not very funny. Mommy is getting upset."

"No luck," I said.

"Come out right now," she said. "Come out right this minute, wherever you are, or I'm going to be very angry!" There was no sound except my father coughing from the bedroom.

"Ask your father if he knows," she said.

I went down the hall and knocked softly on the door of his room and peeked in and asked him about the children. He was lying on the bed, staring at the ceiling. He seemed surprised to see me. I went back to tell Annie.

"He doesn't know anything," I said. "He thinks my mother may have taken them to the store with her."

"Well, shit! I want my babies! If she's taken them, I'll never forgive her."

"Don't be silly. If she did, I'm sure she did it inadvertently. They'll probably come waltzing in any minute."

"How could any adult be so thoughtless?"

"Maybe she called out and we didn't hear her. You were in the shower and I was outside talking to my father."

"Something terrible is happening, and I don't like it. What are we going to do now?" Her face looked so tense and desperate, I hugged her and patted her back.

"Just calm down," I said. "Maybe they walked down to the playground my father was telling them about." She jerked free and started out the door.

"Wait a minute," I said, "and I'll find out where it is."

We drove to the playground, a big, open patch of lawn surrounded by freshly painted yellow curbing and a steel fence. There were some swings and teeter-totters and a Jungle Gym, but the place was completely unpopulated except for one woman with a toddler. Annie jogged over to ask her if she might have seen any other children in the area, but the woman was no help one way or the other. Annie collapsed back onto the seat and moaned.

"Maybe they were on their way home and got lost somewhere in the subdivision," I said.

"Maybe they were kidnapped by some homicidal maniac," she said.

"Oh, for God's sake." She raised her knees up from the seat and started to sob loudly into the folds of her skirt.

"Where are they?" she sobbed. "I want my babies." We cruised several streets around the playground and around my parents' house.

"Keep your eyes peeled," I said. "They might be along here anywhere."

We drove back to the small brick house, number 427, and parked in the driveway and plodded inside. Annie wanted me to call the police. I offered to drive to the grocery store to see if I could find my mother. My father was still in his bedroom lying down. "She'll be back in a few minutes," he said. "I wouldn't worry, Annie."

"If she has taken those children," she said, "I'm leaving this house and never coming back." She went into the guestroom and slammed the door.

"I'm sure Mom didn't intend anything by it," my father said. "Annie'll feel better as soon as they get back."

"She's awfully upset," I said.

"Is she having her period?" he whispered.

"I'm not sure," I whispered back. "It was a long trip, and we didn't sleep very well last night." I went into the front room and sat on the couch and looked out the window. The day was perfectly still, the dust motes floating slowly above the floral slipcover. There was something depressing about the small radiant lawn, the sameness of the houses, the occasional car laboring past the door, oblivious to the lives here, oblivious to the sick old man lying quietly alone in his bedroom, listening to his own heartbeat to be certain it was still functioning, licking the corners of his mouth to be certain he was still alive.

In a few minutes, the white Oldsmobile pulled up in front of the house with my mother behind the wheel, and the kids' heads could be seen bobbing up and down in the backseat. I went out to help my mother with the grocery sacks. I picked up my five-year-old son in one arm and some groceries in the other and said, "Where have you been? We've been looking all over the place for you guys."

"Oh," my mother said. "We just went for a little trip to the store."

"Annie's awfully upset," I said. "She didn't know what had happened to the children."

"They just went along for the ride," my mother said.

"You should have mentioned it to someone before you left. We've been fairly frantic around here looking for them."

"Oh, for heaven's sake—they were perfectly safe. They were with me the whole time."

"That's not the point, Sweetheart. You should have warned someone. . . . You guys go in and see Mama," I said to the kids. "She was worried about you." They bolted eagerly toward the house.

"I thought you saw us leave together," my mother said.

"Nope, no one did. We didn't know what had happened to them."

"Well, for heaven's sake. I must have forgotten. I'm not used to having small children around the house these days, you know. I just didn't think. It'll take me a while to get back in practice."

I picked up another bag of groceries and balanced it on my knee and slammed the trunk lid. "I hope Annie will be all right now that you're back," I said. "She was about to go crazy."

"Oh, for heaven's sake," she said again. "Surely she'll be all right now. I took good care of them. They weren't in any danger at all. I didn't let them out of my sight."

After Annie and I talked it over, we decided to leave the next morning. She was ready to leave then and there, but I argued that this would seem impolite. Not half as impolite as going off with her children and not telling anyone, she said. My parents were very disappointed when I told them our plans. "You just got here," my father said.

"I know," I said, "but it really is a strain with the kids and everything. They're bound to be noisy and restless at their ages; and your dog gets so excited, it probably isn't good for him."

"I just bought a whole houseful of groceries," my mother said, "and now no one will be here to eat them."

"You'll be able to eat them eventually," I said.

"All I ever get to eat is pills," my father said. "I have to take nine pills four times a day, and most of them are as big as pullet eggs."

"I'll apologize to Annie again," my mother said. "It was just a little misunderstanding. I thought she understood. I didn't mean anything by it."

"I know you didn't, Sweetheart."

"Why does she want to go then?" my mother said.

"You *won't* apologize to her," my father said. "*She's* the one who ought to apologize."

"She just thinks it would be better for everyone," I said. "We haven't been sleeping well, the kids are antsy, and Dad's a lot sicker than we realized before we came."

"Annie never has liked me," my father said. "I've tried every way in the world to win her over, but the harder I tried, the more she hated me."

"I wouldn't say that," my mother said.

"And here I am on my deathbed," my father said, "and she pulls something like this. I should have expected it."

"She doesn't hate *you*," my mother said. "I'm the one she's upset with, but I thought she accepted my apology."

"Nobody hates anybody," I said. "We've had quite a good visit except for the snafu about the kids, and she'll get over that. Let's not worry about it and make accusations. That'll only make things worse."

"Why don't you just stay one more day then," my mother said, "and give us a chance to make up for it."

"I think this is the best way to handle it, Sweetheart."

"Tell Annie to come in here," my father said. "I want to talk to her face to face."

"She's lying down right now," I said. "She's not feeling very well."

"I think she's afraid to look me in the eye," my father said.

"Maybe a little later," my mother said.

"When it comes right down to it, she's afraid to see the damage she's done," my father said. A tear rolled down his left cheek.

"Oh, don't be silly," my mother said.

He reached over and took me by the hand. "I'll tell you one thing, Son. This is one helluva way to behave at a time like this. In case you didn't know it, I'm a dying man. This is the last time you or Annie or anyone else is going to see me alive."

"Oh, Dad. Don't talk that way," my mother said. "Now you're getting melodramatic."

"It's true," he said. "Every word of it. You'd better get a good look at me now because—I know I'm not a pretty sight—but this will be the last time you'll ever lay eyes on me outside my funeral." Tears were streaming down both his cheeks.

"Now you've gone too far," my mother said. "We'll talk it over later. I think you'd better get some rest now." She patted him on the shoulder and we left the bedroom.

Outside, she whispered to me: "He gets a little overly emotional sometimes." I nodded. "He doesn't mean anything by it. It's just part of his condition."

"It's all right," I said.

Except to say goodbye the next morning, that was the last time I saw my father alive. My next trip back to Cincinnati, seven months later, was made to attend his funeral. My mother picked me up at the airport.

She said he kept looking at her and the dog the day he died as if he *knew*. He was unable to speak because of the mini-strokes he had had. He would say, "Wait a minute," and pause expectantly, hoping for more words to flow, but nothing would come out. This, from a man who had never in his life been at a loss for words. While he was staring at her and the dog on his last day, mute, zombie-like, small tears trickled from his eyes.

When his heart stopped and he fell from the edge of the bed, he bruised his forehead, cheek, and nose. The funeral director cautioned my mother not to kiss him or touch his face at the funeral or the make-up might rub off those spots.

Perhaps because he had decided at the end on a military funeral, my mother spent every spare second sorting through old papers and boxes, searching frantically for his Honorable Discharge, which she could not find. She was so businesslike, so distracted, so tuned out, that she nearly succeeded in repressing what was happening to her.

The room at the funeral home was so large that I was certain, when I first saw it, that we would stand there for hours staring at the white walls and the coved ceilings, casting an occasional blurry glance in the direction of the silver casket at the far end and feeling embarrassed and miserable, but an overwhelming number of people began arriving and soon the room was bustling with guests. Most of them I had never met, though many of the names were familiar. It should have been no surprise to me that my father had been an extremely popular man, whom many people admired or credited with helping them in business or with personal problems, but I was surprised nonetheless.

The body in the coffin was that of a thin man with a mustache, a stranger. He bore a closer resemblance to the neighbor I had never met than to my father. But I tried my best to appreciate the truth of the matter rather than the appearance. At the conclusion of visiting hours, several obese volunteers from the local Masonic Lodge lined up and read stupidly from a prepared ceremony. After everyone had gone, I spent some time alone with him. The funeral director had to ask me to leave.

In the church the next morning, along with a core of relatives and friends from the day before, half a dozen Marines in full dress uniform were present and accompanied us to Woodlawn Cemetery.

The sort of pomp and circumstance that would have embarrassed my father as a younger man must have seemed necessary in the end to shore up his weakening grasp on his identity. He wanted to be remembered as a man whose life had counted, and, I suppose, when he looked back over his life, his time as a Marine must have seemed the best proof of actions that had made a difference in the world.

I thought of the print on the wall above his desk, which he dutifully took down and nailed up again in every new house we moved into: the Marines raising the flag at Iwo Jima and the inscription: "Here Marine courage and skill were put to the supreme test."

My mother and I stood at his graveside in Ohio in the drizzle while the Marines fired three shots into the gray sky and lifted the flag from his coffin and folded it. "By order of the Commandant of the Marine Corps and the Secretary of the Treasury," one said, "we present you with this flag on behalf of a grateful nation."

• • •

The day my father taught me to drive the tractor, we were alone together in a freshly plowed forty-acre field in Bloomville. He often let me sit between his knees on the front edge of the tractor seat and put my hands on the wheel and pretend to drive while his larger, surer hands did the actual steering. This day he showed me how to make large circles with the grater attached on the back, chopping all the large clods of earth into smaller and smaller lumps. After he had done it several times, he let me sit by myself in the big tractor seat and he hung on behind and I could feel the pressure of his hand on the seat as I made a wide circle the way he had done, steering carefully and overlapping with the previous swath. After I had completed a round or two, my father stepped off the back of the tractor without my knowing it and I made one complete pass alone, thinking he was still there, and when I looked up I was astonished to see him standing in the field ahead of me, grinning and congratulating me.

I prepared for fifteen years for his dying—from the time of his first heart attack—and yet I was caught off guard by his death and, even now, in some way, I am not ready to accept it.

He believed in the American dream with an innocence and fierceness that, at twenty, I took to be corny and mindless. Yet, in middle age, I can see it was the well-earned patriotism of a man who had made brutal, verifiable sacrifices in the name of national honor and for the sake of values about which no civilized person would quarrel.

He had navigated the Depression as a young man and subsequently feared unemployment all his life, especially after forty, yet he quit enough good jobs to have kept a small army happily employed. He worked his way up several avenues of business and having reached a kind of pinnacle or dead end in each instance, quit and moved on to something new. He made and spent two or three fortunes during his lifetime and died a poor man, so poor he was afraid he could not afford the heart operation he needed to stay alive for a few more years.

He loved me with a kind of helpless, unselfconscious paternal devotion that was like a protective mantle, a powerful light always flowing around my shoulders.

When I was a boy we visited the farm often; and although the houses and towns we lived in and the schools I attended from year to year changed and were, in a sense, interchangable, eventually becoming a blur in my memory, the farm was the only location that was always the same, a constant, dependable corner of the earth that I felt I could always refer back to and call my own. The extent to which I made use of this connection was not apparent to me until recently when I visited Bloomville for probably the last time—to attend my grandmother's funeral.

I took an early morning walk down the narrow, humpbacked country road that bisects our land, and I began to notice how many of the sites I passed had secretly lodged in my imagination as vivid and detailed locations for dreams, stories and novels I had read, and automatic reference points to place. This ditch beside the orchard was where I had imagined Sarty Snopes huddled to elude Major DeSpain's horses in "Barn Burning." This small outcropping of trees was where I had imagined the old woman in "Death in the Woods" frozen to death with the sack of food on her back and where the frightened dogs had danced in circles under the moon. For me, I began to realize, Bloomville was Winesburg, Ohio, and Yoknapatawpha County and parts of Updike's Pennsylvania and Flannery O'Connor's Georgia. It was also Cranford and Middlemarch and all of nineteenth-century England.

When we were very small, I remembered, my cousin and I used to dress up in musty old clothes we found in a big trunk in the woodhouse, mainly elegant old lacy dresses and shawls and the silliest hats, and we would come knocking on my grandmother's door, pretending to be old ladies from Bloomville; and my grandmother would welcome us as if she, too, believed we were old ladies and great good friends of hers and she would sit down and pretend to gossip with us.

Both before and after our actual residency there, my father used to invite the men of his family, his brothers and his father, Judge (when he was still alive), and various business acquaintances to visit the farm around Thanksgiving time for the hunting of pheasant and rabbit. I remembered those hunting trips vividly that morning on my walk, possibly because I was looking at some of the same woods and fields they had tramped through so avidly and because I was thinking about final things; and all the members of my father's large family were dead and gone by then, every one of them. But his brothers, my uncles, were a fine bunch of men, stalking the farm in plaid jackets and yellow and fluorescent slickers and heavy boots, shotguns slung under their arms, setting out at daybreak and hunting all day as if their lives depended upon it.

As a small child too young to go along, I remembered wandering out into the summer kitchen and being astonished by three large rabbits, their yellow eyes still clear and open, piled on the wooden deck waiting to be cleaned. I had never seen a dead creature of any kind before that moment, and I remembered staring into their eyes for a long time and feeling an unfamiliar heaviness and sense of anguish. Later on, as I grew older, I was allowed to join in the hunting. I enjoyed the camaraderie and the responsibility of carrying the weapon, but I identified too closely with the animals to ever enjoy the killing. By then, it seemed, there was not much left to kill, anyway. The object seemed to be to tramp for hours across frozen corn stubble or quietly through the trees, to avoid complaining or shooting one another, and to return in the late afternoon to a sumptuous dinner that the women had been cooking since breakfast. That we returned empty-handed did not seem to matter.

Gram's funeral was held on a perfect spring day. Seeing her there, I thought of the irony of my father's oft-repeated remark about her: "She'll probably outlive us all." Well, she was eighty-nine when she died and she did outlive quite a few, including my father. Most of the comments at the funeral from my mother and her sisters were about the flowers, how beautiful they were, as if to avoid the awesome fact of what they surrounded. After hearing the flowers mentioned so many times during the visitation, I noticed during the funeral that they formed a huge, grotesque frame for the casket, and this frame was so unnaturally bright that it almost seemed to be moving toward us like an event in a film, as if to engrave itself and this scene forever on our memories.

In death, I've learned, people resemble themselves somewhat imperfectly. The undertaker, I believe, must have taken it upon himself to smooth out some of Gram's wrinkles. The result was, oddly, that, lying there that day, her most recognizable features were her ears and her arthritic forefinger. Something about that gnarled finger was especially touching—because it reminded us that she had suffered pain? Upon seeing it, my Aunt Olive was moved to remark, somewhat guiltily, that she had once called Gram "old crooked-finger" to taunt her.

Several of the citizens present remembered Dick Townley very clearly and with considerable enthusiasm. A number informed me that they knew I was Dick Townley's son the minute they laid eyes on me. One wanted to know if I was going to come to Bloomville now and be a farmer, but I said no, I was afraid not. The only furrow a librarian is likely to plow is down the middle of a page.

They kept the casket open during the visitation and funeral, and I was dreading the moment during the ceremony when they might close the lid, but they spared us that and did it after we had left. Similarly, at the cemetery, the ceremony was handled in such a way as to deflect strong emotional response. The grave was not even visible. The casket was mounted above it in an imposing metal chassis and so surrounded by flowers that the only evidence of loam at all was the rich smell of it. The entire gravesite was covered by a bright green awning, as if pitched for a festive lawn party, and the grounds were well manicured for Memorial Day and bright with flags and fresh flowers dotting several of the graves.

While the minister gave the eulogy, I thought of how Gram had spent the last forty years of her life protecting and defending the farm against all intruders, as generations of the Spaldings had done before her, how she would sometimes mention proudly that the original deed had been signed during the presidency of James Monroe. I could see the land in my mind's eye as it had looked when I was a child and my father had stopped the car and pointed eagerly across the marsh and the orchard and the green alfalfa fields to the silver-roofed barns gleaming in the sunlight. Somehow, even then, I came to understand that my own destiny was to be committed to that piece of the earth. But it was only an illusion.

Gram had understood the *call* of the land, that to work the land and to defend the land and to cultivate the harvest *is* a calling. But my grandmother was too possessive and short-sighted. Having borne no sons who might naturally have taken over, nor daughters who wanted to, she made a mistake in driving away the only heir in the next generation who loved the farm the way she did, who had a vision for it and the capacity to carry it through and the will to pass it on.

His instinct during those two years—during what today we would call a mid-life crisis—was to retreat from the chaos of civilization, to return to the simpler ways of his ancestors, who had also once worked the land, in order to perpetuate a legacy and an honorable tradition of husbandry, to leave something to his children that was worth inheriting.He failed at that. Instead, he was swept along by circumstances and by the electric and electronic revolutions of the mid-twentieth century and became, in a sense, their handmaiden. Now that he is gone and his brothers are gone, now that Gram and the farm are gone and all that the generations of my mother's family worked to preserve, I sometimes wonder if there is any evidence left on the face of the earth that any of them ever existed?

The night after Gram's funeral, I had a strange dream: It had been raining for days—severe conditions—the sky would blacken suddenly, and windows would be blown out. I was on my way to have an electrical cord repaired, a part of the electrical system of the house that had been damaged by the storms. Annie and the kids were in some danger. The repairman in the shop looked familiar, but I couldn't place him. He was wearing a brightly polished silver space helmet. Later, I realized it was Cooley's former college roommate from the Baylor track—somehow he had found his way into my dream.

On my way home, I got hopelessly lost and I stopped the car along the highway next to this out-of-the-way roadhouse or tavern with the idea of locating someone to ask directions. The building was painted dark green and seemed boarded up, but a large faded sign near the door read: BLOOMVILLE. The place looked abandoned from the outside but, once inside, I could see a tremendous crowd of people in the dining room, eating and talking, smoke rising and glasses clinking and loud laughter.

As I was passing through an aisle near the bar on my way to try to flag down the cashier, I saw a man who bore an uncanny resemblance to my father, sitting at one of the tables. I couldn't resist walking a little closer and looking at him intently. Just as I was passing quite close to him, he turned and looked at me. His light eyes and the shape of his cheeks were unmistakable. His eyes focused on me and instantly he recognized me—it *was* my father, very much alive (he looked about fifty—and was clean shaven and healthy).

My father was sitting with a woman, quite young and pregnant, who was obviously *with* him. I was shocked. He seemed somewhat surprised and embarrassed but immediately said, "Hello, pal," and welcomed me, introducing me to the woman. He was glad to see me, it seemed, though it wasn't going to be easy to explain how he had gotten here, why he hadn't really died, and why he had kept himself concealed from my mother and me for such a long time. He was getting ready though, evidently, to tell me what had happened and it was going to be a good story: who the woman was, where he had been for the last several years and why, how his health had improved so markedly.

Then suddenly we were out beside the road, and I could see him running along the shoulder up ahead, running unbelievably well for his age, and I was frightened that my mother might see him. How would he ever explain to her what he was going to explain to me? And how had he been living here all this time, so near us, and we hadn't chanced upon him before? But then I began to notice that he was outdistancing me. I ran harder to catch up, but I kept falling farther behind. I wanted so much to talk to him, to hear his incredible story. I found I was locked in an all-out sprint, gaining on him slightly but gasping for breath. But he disappeared up ahead around a bend in the road, his arms pumping smoothly, his feet rising and falling in perfect cadence along the sloping highway.

A NOTE ABOUT THE AUTHOR

Joe David Bellamy won the Editors' Book Award for his novel *Suzi Sinzinnati* (Pushcart, 1989; Penguin USA, 1991), and *Atomic Love* is an AWP Award Series selection for short fiction. His fiction has appeared widely in literary magazines, has been cited or reprinted in *The Best American Short Stories, The Pushcart Prize,* and *New Directions* anthologies, and has been supported by grants from the New York State Council on the Arts and from the National Endowment for the Arts. His other books include *The New Fiction, American Poetry Observed,* and *Superfiction;* and two books of poetry, *Olympic Gold Medalist* and *The Frozen Sea.*